The Day
in
Shadow

BY THE SAME AUTHOR

Nayantara Sahgal

The Day in Shadow

W·W·NORTON & COMPANY·INC· NEW YORK

Library of Congress Cataloging in Publication Data

Sahgal, Nayantara (Pandit) 1927–
    The day in shadow.

    I. Title.
PZ4.S13Day 3   823   72–1432
ISBN 978-0-393-33222-3

PRINTED IN THE UNITED STATES OF AMERICA

1 2 3 4 5 6 7 8 9 0

To
Nonika, Ranjit, and Gita

The Day
in
Shadow

1

The huge mirrors of the Zodiac Room at the Intercontinental, festooned in carved gilt, reflected everyone of consequence in the Ministry of Petroleum, and a lot of other officials besides. And their wives. And some of their daughters—the supple, flat-stomached young, with their saris tied low showing their navels, their hair swinging long and loose, or piled high in glossy architecture. They were all enjoying the hospitality of Oil Products Limited. Simrit hazily took in the massed flower arrangements on polished mahogany, trays of elegant little canapes piped in curls of cream arranged on a snowy white cloth at the far end of the room, the hot snacks and fruit juice being passed by white-coated bearers. With the Minister of State for Petroleum expected, no liquor could be served, one of the quaint little hypocrisies enshrined in public life—an interesting sidelight for anyone who cared to make a study of Indian character, Hindu character, Raj would say. The facets and sworls, the thousand and one crevices and folds of Hindu character. The rock against which psychology foundered. It was a favourite subject of Raj's. Almost his obsession.

Simrit recognized names and faces, some connecting in her mind with other parties in the past. After all, she must know a number of people here. No one could spend years in Delhi, even outside officialdom, without coming up against it. But the effort of catching up with acquaintances, like most effort nowadays, was too much to make, and parties like this one, reminders of the husband-centered world she had forsaken, were so unreal.

Raj had an idea she should get out of the house more often, meet more people. Raj was ruthless about life, saying one had to live it aggressively. Simrit caught sight of herself in a mirror, looking like a loser, her own rose shot silk sari draping a ghost—no match for the alive and effervescing company around her. Raj looked very much a part of it, thirty-nine years young, standing against a mirror on the opposite side of the room. She could see two of him gesturing as he talked, scooping up the air around him in generous handfuls like an energetic conductor, his shoulders hunched a little as they were when he concentrated. Now he was helping himself to nuts from a tray on the marble-topped table behind him and making a meal of them from what she could see. In contrast the man he was talking to looked as if he were standing at attention, so neat, contained and motionless was he next to Raj. She remembered Raj telling her that N. N. Shah had the supreme composure of a man who operates a large expense account. Nirvana today was an expense account, the state of bliss where the price rise left you untouched. Som, her ex-husband, had had one too, only it had not given him much poise, never become natural to him. It had hung around him, a thrilling, troubling presence. Som and his money had stayed in two separate compartments, never settling down comfortably with each other.

Simrit smiled back at the people near her, hoping they would not draw her into their conversation, though she recognized Joshi in the group. Delhi was a place where a civil servant's reputation need not have much to do with merit, developing instead in a cloudy haze of good English diction and good manners. The civil servant's traditional anonymity had over the years been replaced by a vague unobtrusiveness, characteristic of an atmosphere from which decision and daring had disappeared, along with efficiency. In this twilight Joshi was the kind of non-personality who stayed out of trouble and survived. He had risen step by step to, within a year of retirement, the take-off point where, unless he did something startling, or the belligerent new politicians had their way and wiped out his kind by an act of legislation, he might become a State Governor or an Ambassador. Simrit had met him when he was Joint Secretary to the Industries Ministry, during Som's efforts to start a new plant. She now put his kindly, enquiring look down to the fact that he had not liked Som.

Som's unpopularity kept cropping up and surprising her. Her Brahmin parents with their instinctive withdrawal from anything outside the fold had been frankly upset at her choice of a businessman husband, but her friends had not liked him either. They had thought him a boor. People

3

always disliked and distrusted commercial flash and flair if they did not possess it themselves. A man had to be flashy on a big scale to be thought well of, and majestically vulgar to be admired, and Som had not arrived in that category. But his flash was what had charmed her, contrasting so vividly with her solitary, book-loving childhood. Som was colour and life and action. All the same, whatever had flourished in her had done so away from his vividness, in hiding from it. They had got on easily enough on the surface, and that had created a game of its own in which intensity, depth and devotion were never brought into play at all. Nor was partnership. Som, the rougher element, had led. Not that she had wanted to lead, only to be, though that would have meant a battle—and she had never been prepared to fight.

"Well, my dear," said Joshi, "how very nice to see you. How is—how are the children?"

He was studying her solicitiously, as if divorce were a disease that left pock marks.

"You must come and see us," he went on. "I'll give you a ring. Have you a telephone?"

No telephone. And a ration card and even a milk card for the Delhi Milk Scheme would take weeks to get. And there were bottles and bottles of milk to be bought for the children. Of course she could get dairy milk at market prices but the Government milk was cheaper.

"No, I haven't a telephone. I haven't applied for one yet, and I expect it will take ages when I do."

Eight years, she had heard. The only thing you could get without a hitch was a divorce. Well, it took two years actually; but that was phenomenally quick when it took a year to get a Birla car, four or five to get a Fiat, and all eternity, according to Som, to get a licence to manufacture something. You'd think there would be some sense of proportion about it and that the break-up of a family would be a little harder to accomplish. But no, you could get a divorce by mutual consent at the drop of a hat. The Hindu Code Bill had jumped two thousand years of tradition to confer that particular twentieth-century blessing. And here we are, she thought, the females among us, in a state of revolutionary emancipation, out on our ears in the street. It had been by consent—of a sort—but the recollection brought so much tumult with it that she quickly banished it from her mind.

Joshi's concern was very welcome.

"Let me see if we can hurry up a telephone for you. You write, don't you?"

She nodded.

"Well then there's an entitlement under the journalists' quota. I'll see what I can do."

"But I'm not an accredited journalist," she said, "and I don't write regularly for the newspapers."

Accreditation would have been the answer to a number of her problems. It would have got her a telephone and precious controlled-rent accommodation. In Delhi a label went a long way. And here she was rattling around without one.

Joshi frowned, "Then it's more complicated. But I think it can be managed. I'll let you know."

He wrote down her address.

"Let me introduce you to some friends of mine."

He took her carefully by the elbow and guided her toward the group near them. Two bland, smooth-faced women indifferently acknowledged the introduction.

"You live in Delhi?"

"Yes," said Simrit.

She steeled herself for the next question.

It came. "Where do you live?"

5

Her own vague answer was of someone marooned and not yet sure of her surroundings. "In a flat in Defence Colony."

No number. No block. They were looking at her curiously.

"What does your husband do?" one of them wanted to know.

Wasn't it odd, when you were standing there yourself, fully a person, not to be asked what you did? There was such an enormous separating gulf between herself and these women, most women—most people. Maybe the question would be different in the twenty- first century. Simrit herself had never accepted a world where men did things and women waited for them. Hadn't she? She could hear Raj demanding, never letting her get away with any neat hem-stitched notions about herself. Whatever her views on emancipation were, she had kept them well buried.

"I am divorced," she said.

"Oh," said the woman.

"Then you must be working," said her companion.

They had fixed her with a twin Joshi look. It made her feel she had broken out in spots and scales.

"I am a writer."

It sounded so terse and self-advertising.

"Which newspaper do you write for?"

"I free lance. But I don't write much for the newspapers. Only the occasional article."

That was another trouble. She hated talking about things that mattered deeply, particularly when they fell, as they did now, into a polite vacuum. She longed to change the subject to servants, children, or the batik show at the Imperial. Anything but writing. She wished the party would end or that she could disappear from it.

"I have a niece who writes now and then," one of them said, "She writes the cleverest little pieces. It gives her some-

6

hing to do till she marries."

She stopped abruptly.

"Simrit Raman?" the first woman placed her. "I've seen a book by you. It was about a place—a valley, wasn't it, or a stream?"

"A river," said Simrit, tormented.

"A river?"

"Yes," said Simrit.

"But that's very clever."

They smiled. Simrit smiled wanly back. Raj, catching her eye, held up his hand and she thankfully excused herself to cross the room. Everybody had a particular aura, and Raj just then radiated an atmosphere of suppressed jubilation that lapped around her in waves.

"Everything all right?" he demanded. "You look bleak."

She shook her head, tongue-tied.

"Meet our host, Mr Shah, Managing Director, Oil Products Limited —Mrs Raman."

Simrit clasped both hands around her glass of orange juice in an awkward namaskar.

"Mrs Raman, you have written a book about a river," stated Mr Shah. "I have read it. But why about a river?"

"Because rivers are less complicated than human beings," Raj answered for her.

He went on talking cheerfully, covering her silence.

"Do you realize, Simrit, what a lot of things are made of petroleum? Plastics, textiles, cosmetics, soap, this ashtray, this tabletop, I shouldn't wonder."

He ran his hand along its cool green-streaked surface.

"That is quite definitely marble," Simrit managed.

"Oh all right, but almost anything else you can name. Am I right?" he turned to Mr Shah.

Their host inclined a smooth, brilliantined head.

"With the new agreement we have signed today there is no knowing what products we may yet add to that list," he said pleasantly.

He raised his glass to Raj.

"This is an agreement between Government and Oil Products Limited to manufacture petrochemical products," Raj explained to Simrit.

"And very timely too," added Mr Shah in his carefully enunciated English. "In business one must either expand or fold up. One cannot remain static."

"Unlike the Government which can stay static for incredible amounts of time," said Raj.

Mr Shah chuckled appreciatively. He turned to Simrit.

"I have been urging Mr Garg to come into our organization. He would have all the facilities he needs to work out his ideas. After all he cannot remain a Member of Parliament forever."

"But it's only been three years," protested Raj. "I still have two to go."

"And what does he say to your offer?" Simrit asked Shah.

"That he will then be too comfortable and secure, so he cannot join us. Mr Garg is a very unusual man."

"I like my own little headaches," admitted Raj. "If I joined Mr Shah, there wouldn't be any."

Mr Shah's denial was vehement.

"I would not say that. The bigger the organization, the more the headaches. I guarantee you your share. We are not Japan. Now look at Japan. There is a complete meeting of minds between government and business, and the workers work. That is why they prosper and are not plagued with strikes."

"Mr Shah," Raj told Simrit, "looks at Japan with the longing that the devout reserve for paradise."

"And paradise it is compared with us," lamented Mr Shah. "Other countries put their business houses on the honour roll. We treat ours like criminals."

He put down his glass, said he hoped they were enjoying themselves and went away to look after his other guests.

Raj took a gulp of tomato juice, ran his fingers through his hair, and said he wished he had brought a hip flask with him. "What was Joshi scribbling?"

"My address. He's going to help me get a telephone."

"You mean Joshi has committed himself to a course of action?" he grinned.

"Yes, of course he has. What are you looking so excited about anyway, this agreement to produce things?"

"No," said Raj. "Haven't you seen the news? It was in the evening papers. The well the Oil Commission was drilling at Jammu struck oil today. The news was phoned to the Lok Sabha and they interrupted the proceedings to announce it. I've never seen such excitement. Right, Left, Centre, everybody forgot their wrangles. It was like a declaration of war. Electrifying."

"But we have oil wells already. This isn't the first."

Cambay and Ankleshwar had been names in the news years earlier.

"Yes, but piteously little for our requirements. And there's no knowing how much or little this one will produce. But it promises to be a big find."

"I don't understand much about it," she confessed.

"Anything that changes the face of the world has to be understood," said Raj severely.

"I always thought of oil in terms of a handful of millionaires."

"New discoveries keep changing that picture. Countries want to own their own oil. It's dangerous to be dependent on others in such a vital commodity. And independence has no meaning unless it's economic. You're realizing that now yourself."

"Stop tying me up with the Government's economic affairs," said Simrit. "If I'm in a mess, it's my own stupid fault, signing Som's terms without understanding them."

"It's all part of the same thing," said Raj. "Signing on the dotted line is the hallmark of the defeated and the damned, or at least of those who don't have the whip hand, whether they're trusting souls like you or governments without know-how. Take oil, for instance."

There was no time to explain. Flash bulbs popped at the door as Sumer Singh came in, still looking preoccupied with the Cabinet meeting that had delayed him.

If one had to have a label in this city the Minister of State for Petroleum certainly had one. He also had youth, an enviable qualification when most politicians were ageing men, and a romantic background: zamindar turned servant of the people. To top it all he was the hope of the up and coming new radicals in the ruling party and everyone knew it was a matter of time before they took over the party. All that and Gandhi too, for the Mahatma had been a family friend and had stayed in his ancestral home—Gandhi who, paradoxically, had had no quarrel with money or the rich, who had believed that the love and service of the lowly had very little to do with blood on the barricades or slogans renting the sky for earth-shaking causes. Try as she might Simrit could not fit Gandhi and the new radicals together. The Gandhi image sat farcically on the ruling party all right, observed Raj, but it had to be kept there, because no one could yet capture and hold the masses without it.

"They'll dispense with him when they're good and ready," he said, "but meanwhile they'll keep resurrecting him cold-bloodedly — unwinding the mummy — whenever they need him. A more cynical bunch of manipulators would be hard to find."

It was a far cry from the way people generally talked about him, said Simrit, as if he had just walked by and they somehow were better for it.

Raj agreed. Then, though he was not a practising Christian, he said with the trace of wistfulness his manner had when he spoke of the God he did not believe in, "Yes, that's it exactly. I imagine people must once have spoken of Christ like that: Jesus of Nazareth passed this way. I saw him with my own eyes. He drank from this cup. I gave it to him myself. He trod these cobblestones, blessed my child, healed that cripple."

Simrit listening, felt gently lifted out of herself and soothed. It could happen listening to Raj, even in the middle of a reception by Oil Products Ltd. At other times what he said could do more. It could set her free, give her the joyful sensation of climbing a hill with the breeze blowing in her face. Before she'd met Raj she had been part of a frieze, one of those elaborate wooden ones in old temples with figures minutely carved in them. Raj had uncarved her. But maybe a figure in a freize belonged in a frieze. It wasn't even good art all by itself, only a common bit of wood. Most of the time she felt like that.

Raj continued, "There are rare times when ordinary people get linked with big events, when intimate and personal affairs get mixed up with the stupendous, when a person can say: I was there. It happened to me. That's what makes living legend out of the dry stuff of history. It obviously happened to people in the time of Christ, and with Gandhi here. Only Jesus of Nazareth left a Church behind him, men and women to carry on the good work, and Gandhi this absurd Liliputian ilk, inflated with office, and unerring in its attack on the wrong things."

Som's world had been commerce, never shared with her at all. And here was politics, utterly confusing. The imposing red sandstone buildings where all government debate and activity centered had been to her just buildings until Raj had started investing them with a huge snarled personality. Delhi had been simply home, a place to bring up children, but apparently it was much more, a touchstone for whatever happened in India. Delhi could become the heart of a crisis.

"And it will," he worried, "if they keep spinning out their slogans while millions queue up for jobs."

The country, he said, had once been help together by be lief as radiant as the sun. Now nobody knew where the seat of actual power was. There were so many little tides, and so many little planets orbited. Even the Minister of State for Petroleum was unbelievably one of them. How he had become a rising star in the political firmament was a mystery. But a photogenic profile did not seem nearly enough qualification for the difficult decision-making that awaited his Ministry. And today's news made the question of what calibre of man Sumer Singh was very important.

Simrit found herself watching the Minister of State as closely as she could in inadequate glimpses through a screen of guests. He was as different as could be, everyone said, from the senior Minister lying ill in hospital, whom he was representing here today. When the crush around Sumer Singh thinned they could see him better, decorously sipping his orange juice, listening attentively to his host, using his eyes like a woman while he acknowledged with a smile and a namaskar those who greeted him. It was hard to say how far he was astute politician, how far just glamour boy.

"Wonder what he's like when no one's watching," said Raj.

But he was always wondering what "they" were like, what, if anything, "they" believed in. He was back to his favourite quarrelling point—the Hindus. The Hindus, according to him, had no belief they could define or defend; they just had an endless spongelike capacity to absorb. The sponge had been all right, necessary in fact for survival when for hundreds of years they had been up against the sword of Islam and then the British. But now why did no one show his face, his mind, his objective, if he had one?

"If I worked for this government, I'd go mad," said Raj.

"You make too much of it," said Simrit.

"Do I?" he was amazed. "Surely enough isn't made of it. This whole question of what a Hindu stands for has yet to be sorted out. No one has begun to do it."

The Christian Church talked about the mystery of Christ but what baffled him was the enigma of Hinduism. Christianity was clear and classic in its simplicity, a belief that could be translated into life and action and give meaning to each day — if one believed. But Hinduism couldn't be turned into action at all, worse, it could become inhuman action. What other religion sanctioned that a man shun contact with his own kind, with another Hindu? And that was only one aspect of the enigma. Until this and other uglinesses were forced out and millions of ordinary people found a working philosophy, a decent one for every day, how would the country's problems be solved?

"Raj, I have to go home. It's late," said Simrit.

Sumer Singh caught sight of them as they reached the door and raised his eyebrows in recognition of Raj. Raj indicated with a gesture that he had to leave.

They came out into the lobby. It was brimming with

new arrivals, the winter tourist influx into Delhi, with their tiers of smart new suitcases with foreign tags. They would go to Agra and Jaipur, said Raj, ride on elephants, look at the Taj and jet home. And not one dollar-dripping one of them would know that today might change the face of India.

"You mean that oil discovery?" asked Simrit.

"What else?"

Raj stopped in the middle of the lobby to exclaim over her ignorance, attracting several amused glances.

"We should celebrate, Simrit. Let's have dinner here, up on the top where we can see all the lights of Delhi. I'll be ruined for the rest of the month but never mind. Or better still, let's collar Shah and make him foot the bill."

"Shah has his party to look after and I have to go home. The children are waiting."

"The children can look after each other. We can phone."

"I don't have a phone," she reminded him.

Raj accepted defeat. They went through the glass doors of the lobby out into the entrance where Raj asked the doorman to call a taxi.

"Did you enjoy the party?" he asked after telling the driver to take them first to her flat in Defence Colony.

Away from the bright lights Simrit felt depression closing in.

"How can I enjoy anything? I can't even begin to think straight till things are settled at the flat." She had moved in so recently, it was not yet home. "I feel so disorganized."

"That's the way you may have to live for a while yet. Be patient, Simrit. It's how we'll have to live in this country for years yet, in a bit of a mess, with things not in their places, and not nearly enough of them to go round. And we'll have to learn to love the process, to get something out of it and go on giving something to it. There are no magic formulas. We can't make coaches out of pumpkins except by our sweat, and that takes time."

It was all very well for the country, she thought tiredly, but what about *her* life? A small wail started in her whenever she thought of *that*, she who loved order and beauty excessively and not because she had been born to them. They were her trade. She could never understand the theory that writers and artists were untidy people glorying in chaos. How could she whose working hours were spent struggling to give fine structure to the unformed, putting ideas into clear language, chiselling precise sentences and paragraphs from a welter of feeling, not be disciplined? Not that it mattered now when the chaos was inside her. She couldn't order it by putting chairs and tables, or even painfully ground out sentences into place — though it helped. Somehow, obscurely, it helped.

Raj was restless, lighting a cigarette, winding the window glass down to throw away the match and up again. She sensed he would have been more comfortable behind the wheel. He hated not doing things for himself.

"And Simrit, you simply have to start enjoying yourself."

"How can I?" she burst out in anguish.

"You have to try. You can't give up because you're tired or wretched."

"You're always threatening to resign your seat in Parliament," she pointed out.

Raj said immediately, "But I wouldn't, you know."

She knew he would not. Raj felt he was responsible for India. It was almost his personal possession, in turn his delight and his devastation. That was the bond they shared. It had been such a shock coming upon it, this compelling passion so like her own for the thing that mattered more to her than any other. And besides, it was astonishing how he

15

looked at life, as if all of it still lay ahead of him. She wondered if she could be like that ever again, look ahead, make decisions, actively *be*, instead of just getting past each day, feeling as if large pieces of her had been cut out with scissors, with an icy wind blowing through the gaps. Raj was so blessedly whole with a personality that stood out distinct as rock on a flat landscape. With Raj "yes" meant "yes" and "no" meant "no." "The Christian in me," he would mock. She had come to rely on him more and more since she had set up on her own in Defence Colony. He always did what he said he would do, the only stable element in the emotional debris of her new world. He was solidly there. As the taxi drew up to the gate of the double-storeyed building where she lived, she felt deadened at the prospect of Raj driving away, taking his rich warm concern with him. Yet she had never been prepared to do more than quietly accept it. And he, normally so assertive, even domineering, seemed to hold back deliberately when it came to her, as though waiting for a sign from her—one that she had lost the capacity to give.

She unlocked her door and stood in the entrance, filled with unreasoning dread, as if an assassin waited there in the dark for her. She switched on the light and the uncurtained, naked-looking room with its bare minimum of furniture looked blankly back at her—another unformed thing she would have to shape and tend the next day and the next, until it gave back something of its own. The very thought was intimidating.

From a room down the corridor came the sound of a muffled sneeze. It was her youngest child, who insisted on covering her head with a blanket when she slept. Simrit smiled. She came into her flat more confidently now, closing the door behind her, and went down the corridor to the room where the little children lay breathing evenly in their sleep. There was no beginning and no end. One always came in somehow in the middle, with jobs needing to be done. Events flowed away into the past and the future, lived through and yet to come, and to belong to them one had to find a firm foothold now, in the present.

Sounds of laughter came from the other bedroom, the only properly furnished one, where the big children must be waiting for supper. They were already eating when she went in to be greeted with cries and questions.

"What was the party like, Mama?"

Her son got up to take her coat. Simrit's eyes rested on each of them in turn and she had to close them to accustom herself to the radiant assault of their love and attention. She sat down in the place they made for her and began to eat and talk at the same time. After they had gone to bed she stood on the balcony outside her room. Uncut grass growing as it liked, stubby in places, unruly with weeds in others, lay lacquered black in the night, open to dew and stars. Dark shapes of trees, hedge and foliage flocked round it softly like friendship in another form. She felt embraced by a pervasive and purifying calm that nothing human could provide. The best moments were these, possessing like the night a quality of eternity, when she could become part and parcel of the universe and prey no longer to the fears and hungers of the instant.

She went back to her room, and undressed slowly, thinking of her first meeting with Raj two years earlier at a discussion on current events. All the participants, wellknown men and women in teaching, journalism and government, had seemed to want to hear the sounds of their own voices, not elicit some conclusions from their combined experience. She, always timorous in a gathering, had kept quiet. It was after a senior Secretary to Government had spoken for five minutes with wonderful fluency, revealing no opinion, that Raj had interjected a judgment. That was what it had sounded like, a judgment—not a summing up so much as a ringing statement of what had been wrong with the discussion. In a few emphatic sentences he had declared that their opinions were borrowed. There was an intellectual vacuum a hundred and fifty years old to be filled in the country and it had to be filled by people who thought for themselves. "When we start thinking about what civilization owes to India," he had said, "we have to go back to 500 B.C. This race has yet to produce a modern thesis of its own."

He proceeded to reject the "borrowed" ones. He spoke briefly of the "sublime theory of Communism" but of the blood on its hands that must outlaw it as the choice of civilized people. He told them of his own impassioned socialism but of the changing and defining it needed to get it to work. "Most of us are socialists," he said, "but what does it mean?" It was time to put this emotional notion into the laboratory of Indian conditions—and find out what part of it was useful and what was waste. When he sat down there was a complete silence. Simrit held her breath. He had not used an unnecessary word or raised his voice by a half tone—she who was used to fist thumping and command, noticed that—but what he had said had been commanding. It had had the effect of revealing the horizon.

That ardent emphasis belonged to the young with the future in their eyes, she had thought, not to the getting on in life like all of us. He had looked directly at her just then and smiled.

He came up behind her at the entrance where she waited for her car.

"The meeting seemed to break up like a biscuit after your

pronouncement," she said.

He was amused by the simile.

"Yes, didn't it? But why a biscuit?"

"It was rather crumbly anyway, and what you said sort of disintegrated it."

"I didn't mean to do that—though the discussion didn't seem to be getting anywhere. Biscuit-variety definitely! And what a self-satisfied collection of people. Not a seeker among them. We don't seem much prone to lightness."

"I wonder why," said Simrit.

"I suppose it's because the Hindus have such a fully developed assurance that everything will always be as it was, forever and ever amen. They will assimilate everything they encounter and reproduce it as an offshoot of themselves. So nothing is either a danger or a challenge."

"The Hindus?"

She was not accustomed to the delineation, to being singled out. One could single out the Muslims or the Sikhs or the Christians for comment, but not the Hindus any more than one could casually refer to the Himalayas as mounds when they were mammoth mountains. The Hindus were not a group, they were a mass, *the* mass. They had no beginning. They had always been. She said so to Raj.

He was leaning against a wall laughing, she felt, at her. "That was just my point," he said.

It was such an attractive sound that she was glad she had taken special trouble with her appearance. She tucked a strand of blowing hair into place behind one ear.

"Even the sun, moon and stars are under analysis today. Everything is, except Hinduism," said Raj. "How do you explain that?" She was still trying to sort it out when he asked, "Are you waiting for a taxi? I can give you a lift."

Her car drew up as he spoke, the one Som's company had

lately bought from the STC, long and shining red, flaunting its privilege and foreignness in the Delhi traffic. The chauffeur stood holding the door open for her.

"I beg your pardon," said Raj with exaggerated reverence while the chauffeur waited impassively, the door still held open.

Simrit felt very young and gay.

"I would prefer a lift with you," she said, "if you have time."

She instructed the chauffeur to take the car back to Som's office.

"We were not introduced," she said, "but I am Simrit Raman."

"Yes I know. Someone at the meeting told me. I hoped you'd say something."

"I'm not very good at that."

They walked to the car park and she got in beside him. All the way they talked easily about random things, the exquisite balmy weather, the discussion group.

"The trouble with us," said Raj, "is that we haven't discovered ourselves. There are the Russia-lovers among us and the America-lovers, and though it's a dwindling group, the sentimental bunch midway who still want everything from education to defence equipment from Britain rather than strike out in fresh markets, get newer techniques and make better bargains, and between the lot of them something vital is being drained away, apart from what it costs us in mistakes. What we need is a new breed of India-lovers."

In no time they were home. She was glad the children were all there, streaking down the road on bicycles, swinging on the gate. Simrit's fifteen-year-old daughter came with carefully cultivated poise to greet them and be introduced to Raj. The others gathered round and stared. Afterwards Simrit thought it was very nearly the last time she had seen them so spontaneous and unshadowed.

"Who's he?" demanded her youngest.

Simrit took the little girl's hand and held it, happy with the feel of it and the soft bright afternoon.

"My name," said Raj, "is Raj Edwin Garg."

"Why has he got an English name in the middle?" the child cut in.

"That's a long story," said Raj. "I'll tell you about it some time."

"I live not very far up the road from you," he told Simrit, giving her his address. "Please drop in when you feel like it, both you and your husband."

But it was a long time before she had, and Som had never gone at all.

2

Som had not liked going out, so invitations from her friends had tapered off. It puzzled Simrit who had thought him gregarious. He did have all the right ingredients—the ready laughter, the energy, loving to eat and drink—but they did not make him outward. Actually he was a secret person. Suppose he robbed a bank or committed a crime, she found herself thinking, how would I feel about him?

Som, out of his bath, was towelling himself vigorously in front of the dressing-table mirror, pleased with his muscular, not-an-extra-ounce figure. A fine physical specimen he was, but it needed some slight imperfection, a chink in the armour to awaken her tenderness.

"Ghastly mirror," he said. "It's all distorted down one side. God, how I hate this dingy house and all its trappings."

He was a junior executive in Lansdowne and Co., the second job he had had since they had married, and the house wasn't bad. It was old-fashioned with its high ceilings and uneven floors. Not smart, but it had plenty of room for the children. And Simrit had persuaded him not to change the furniture.

"The Company china is hideous!" he went on. "So is the Company linen. God knows how many people have used it before us. We'll buy our own. We can afford it."

In some ways Som was more like a woman and she like a man. The china and linen were all right. They did not bother her a bit.

"One of these days we're going to have our own monogrammed china and linen."

Simrit giggled at the idea, and Som turned to face her.

"My dear girl, one has to know what one wants and plan for it."

"Yes I know."

"And it's time we started a cellar. I intend to put away wine for my son's coming for age."

"Where are you going to get the wine from? And you have daughters too," Simrit pointed out.

"I'm already putting shares in his name."

Brij ran into the room. Som picked him up and tossed him high into the air, singing: "My son, my son, you're going to be very very rich."

Brij shrieked with the thrill of it. When he was put down he rushed out shouting to his sisters.

"He would have had twice as much," said Som, "if we hadn't lost so much at Partition. Poor chap. You would have

23

had twice as much too."

He began to describe his father's collection of carpets, his mother's jewellery, her favourite piece, a heavy gold necklace of intricate workmanship with bracelets to match, lost in the Partition. Looted and destroyed like so much else. They had been lucky to get away with as much as they did, lucky to have an Indian army convoy as protection part of the way.

Her mind filled with the terror and savagery of it while Som described the carpets, Kashmiri and Persian, in the drawing room of the house abaned at Partition, the panelling on the walls, the marble in the foyer. In her mind's eye she saw instead the frantic street outside, the exodus of the completely disinherited trudging toward no imaginable future, with only what they carried or wore.

"And those swine here in Delhi had the nerve to call it freedom," said Som. "Castrated bunch of Gandhi followers."

"Gandhi didn't approve of Partition," said Simrit.

"Makes no difference. All this mess came of Gandhi politics. Plenty would rather have stayed under the British than lose everything in Partition. Result: people like myself have had to start from scratch."

"Oh Som, hardly from scratch!"

"My dear girl, you have no conception what we lost. I could have furnished six houses with the stuff my mother had put away. And Brij—that's what I can't forgive—Brij would have been a millionaire right now. How do I look? Would you say you have a good-looking husband?"

"Very," said Simrit.

He was about to order breakfast when she said hesitantly, "Som, I think I'm pregnant."

He was one of a large family himself but that did not mean he would want more children.

Brushing a hair off his lapel, he said, "Well, I hope it's not

24

boy. One boy is all anyone should have. Brothers always quarrel about money."

It seemed to her a peculiar thing to quarrel about, especially when there was plenty of it. But Som had assured her that half the feuds and litigation in the Punjab were between close relations, often brothers, over land and money. They could go on for generations. People killed for them.

Simrit did not specially want a boy—or another baby. But pregnancy had accidentally spread a feast before them, a lavish flowering sensuality that took all the time in the world to fulfil itself. It transformed Som, making him a little afraid and beautifully unsure. After the baby came he would go back to imprisoning them within the act, but while this lasted she made the most of it. She never told him she felt reckless, not fragile, during those months.

Back from a walk that evening she went through the house calling Som's name. The door of his study was closed and she barged in. Som and the man with him did not look at her. They were talking in Punjabi and they went on talking. She closed the door and went to her room. Later she ate and went to bed. Som and the man drank and ate and talked into the night. She could hear them from her room. After that the man came often. She knew him as Lalli.

When Lalli was drunk he sang. Sometimes he and Som sang together, starting lustily, trailing off into groans and laughter. Simrit could picture them, meat and rotis demolished, waiting for the servant to bring them pan. Their late-night conversations were haunted by the homes their parents had been driven from, Lahore and Rawalpindi, soil and folklore foreign to her, places farther northwest than she had ever been, and now were Pakistan. If she burst in on them now, would they even see her, gripped by a past that Som at least scarcely remembered except in certain vivid patches and other

25

people's recollections. Night after night they rebuilt it in jokes and anecdotes till it was more solid than the house they sat in or the life she and Som lived. Lalli and he were locked together in a primitive cement much older, more enduring than marriage. Ancestral, tribal, village cement, to which she was a stranger. What she and Som had was the upper layer, floating free. The thought of the monogrammed china and linen suddenly frightened her. They were so far from Som's real hunger. It was not too late to make a life that mattered. Som was thinking of a change too, but one along the same road.

"I'm never going to get anywhere with the Company," he announced.

"Why, are you having trouble with them?"

"No, only with that bastard Merriwether."

"But you've always liked Merriwether."

"He's coming here next week on tour and I'm not going to send the car to the airport for him."

"You can't do that, Som."

"Can't I? He didn't send me one when I went to Calcutta in January. I had to take the blasted airlines bus. There was a taxi strike."

"But you aren't entitled to a car. And he's a Director of the Company."

Merriwether had given Som the job and during his visits to Delhi an agreeable mutual relationship had grown up. Som had even become rather fond of him. Besides, Merriwether was a good sort.

"I don't care what he is, I'm leaving the Company." He turned to her impulsively, "It's nothing to worry about, Sim. It's not as if I have to go job-hunting."

She knew he did not have to and that was not what troubled her.

"It's Merriwether—" she began.

"Oh hang Merriwether. D'you think one can get anywhere in a British firm? I'm going into business with Lalli."

He kicked the dressing table. "We'll be rid of this hideous thing and all this old used junk. We're moving out of here into a new house. Lalli's helping."

"But there's no harm in sending the car for Merriwether."

He said emphatically, hard-faced, "No. No car for Merriwether. That's my parting shot."

Lalli called her Bhabi. He and Som still talked to each other in Punjabi in her presence, ignoring her. But Som would squeeze and stroke her arm, rest his hand warmly, heavily, on her thigh, keep her physically in the room, mentally out. She stopped minding the isolation with this skin to skin seduction between them. He would lean over and kiss her cheek with relish as though he were tasting a peach. Lalli's presence made lingering contact a pleasure for Som. She tried to imagine it continuing between her and Som without Lalli. A weekend with Som, somewhere remote, where she would methodically break down his dividing lines, melt one gesture into another, make them soft, searching children with each other. But Som didn't feel the need.

"It's time you married, Lalli. Look what I've got. Good enough to keep under lock and key."

"My tastes are more ordinary," Lalli would grin.

Between the men there seemed perfect uninhibited accord. Their views fitted smoothly, their arguments vehemently supported each other's. They could make a shattering amount of noise, roistering around like schoolboys.

"Out of the way, Sim. I'm going to show this big hulk what real muscle is."

And they would wrestle, evenly matched, laughing and grunting till out of breath one would force the other to his knees and shout victory. She was passing through the room once when Som, flushed with success, swept her off her feet and put her struggling on top of the high book shelf. And both men laughed uproariously at her till she had to join in.

"Lalli's good for you, Som. He's a loyal friend."

"Tremendous."

"How is it he hasn't married?"

"He was. That's why he's in no hurry. He's looking for an ugly woman."

"Whatever for?"

"His first wife was a good looker. He found her in bed with another man, so he shot her. He doesn't want that to happen again."

Simrit gasped. "You're exaggerating. That's murder."

"Lalli's a loyal man like you said. He expects a loyal wife."

"But how can a man go scot free when he's committed murder?"

"Where he comes from, what a man does with his wife is his private affair. Besides, a lot of things happened during the Partition. Do you think the law matters at a time like that?"

Anyway, it must have been safer to be on Lalli's side than the law's.

"Som, doesn't it give you a strange feeling? I mean, you can't condone murder."

"Look Sim, I understand black and white. Either a woman wants you or she doesn't. It's pretty clear this one didn't want him."

"Yes, but why did he shoot her?"

"Because he only had one damned bullet in his revolver. If he'd had another he'd have shot the scoundrel with her as well. As it is he thrashed him, probably maimed him. Lalli's got hands like raw-hide."

Lalli's and Som's business flourished and Lalli decided to build his own house. He chose the sanitary fittings with special care, and there was quite a ceremony after they were installed, a different coloured tile in each of the three bathrooms, handsome mirrors, gleaming chromium towel rails. Som and Lalli stood in his pink-tiled bathroom drinking their whisky while the children jumped all over the drawing room with no one to restrain them.

"I," said Lalli, looking round his bathroom with satisfaction, "have arrived. Bhabi must take a whisky this evening."

"I've been telling Lalli," said Som to Simrit, "that he'll have to change—start looking more like a sahib and less like a prizefighter—if he wants to be worthy of this bathroom—or he'll crack that fancy mirror when he shaves. And as for him sitting on that, he'll probably break it the first time he sits down. It's a bit delicate looking for the likes of him."

Lalli and Som exchanged a reminiscence and a shout, and thumped each other on the back.

"Drink your whisky, Bhabi," said Lalli, his eyes streaming, "I was telling your husband this is a far cry from the hole in the ground I used in the village where I spent my childhood. Pink tile and all these frills!" and he was convulsed again.

"He's preserved the *lota* he used, to mark the contrast," Som interrupted. "Where is it, Lalli?"

"I have it. But that skinny architect with his refined ways might have had a heart attack if he saw it in his precious bathroom. I was waiting for him to leave." Lalli lovingly produced an old brass lota, its interior metal worn in places, and they drank to it.

It was at a party Lalli gave in the house that they met Rudy Vetter. Vetter was doing business with the government but he was looking for an Indian collaborator for a new line he wanted to start.

"Is he going to join you and Lalli?" Simrit asked.

"Not on your life. We've just got everything going the way we want it. Lalli says you have to be careful with these European bastards. Slippery customers. They want all the advantages their side. They've had it their own way too long in this country."

Lalli and Som invented a name for Vetter. It wasn't very complimentary.

3

There was silence at the table, then suddenly everyone seemed to be talking at once. It happened so often at meals, a manufactured liveliness that drooped and sagged at intervals before it was briskly picked up again. Simrit looked at her children in turn, imagining the ones she did not have, the dozens she might have had, each ensuring tranquility with Som. She pictured a long procession of her unconceived and unborn. One at least might have been like her father, scholarly and gentle-dealing. One surely like her unworldly mother. One might even have been like herself. Funny, none of these was. What was the matter with her genes? These children had all turned out like Som or his family. It was part of the imbalance of her marriage, leaving her unassertive even in reproducing her kind.

Raj, for some reason, sat not at the other end of the table where as the only other adult he should have been seated, but on her right. She did not know how the arrangement had begun but that had become his place whenever he came to dinner.

"Look at you at your age, Mama having to help you," said her youngest with withering scorn, as Simrit put potatoes on Raj's plate.

"Look at you at your age," Raj countered, "fussing over your food."

They eyed each other with suspicion.

"Mama doesn't put more potatoes on my plate," she persisted.

"Oh shut up," commanded her brother, "and eat."

The bickering subsided and there was silence again. Simrit picked up her fork and pushed her food around. She wondered if her children hated Raj or whether the young were just naturally disagreeable when they were uprooted. But *I'm* here, body and soul, she thought, *that* should make some difference.

There were no shades on the lights yet but from the dining alcove where they sat she could now look across the drawing room at new chocolate-coloured net curtains. Their presence helped to dignify the clutter in the room. They hung in prim folds exactly three inches from the floor. The exactitude of the job was consoling. She had taken a chance on a young tailor she had found in the local market yesterday. He had sat here all day measuring, cutting and machining, and finally sewing on hooks and rings with pinpoint precision, stopping only to eat his lunch from a tiny brass tiffin carrier. Order in living, Simrit reflected, happened because people were putting it there, just so many stitches on so much cloth, so much and no more salt in the food, steel on the railroad, brick in the kiln. They all bore the faithful stamp of obedience to purpose. There were crimes of all sorts but none to match deliberate disorder deliberately inflicted— like divorce. It needed a special temperament to live with disorder and not go crazy. Loving the process, Raj called it. Well, someone else would have to love this particular process. She didn't like anything about it, starting with this flat. The flat was all right as flats went. What was wrong was that she and the children should be in it at all.

It looked out across what would have been green grass if someone had taken pains with it. On both sides were flats like hers, neat and compact, with wrought-iron balconies displaying potted plants and wire baskets of flowers. At this hour light filtered through drawn curtains, and there were sounds of Indian and Western music, softly discordant. In Defence Colony where priority plots had been made available to the armed services, rents were a little cheaper than some of the other new housing developments in Delhi, but still too expensive for her. She wondered how long she would be able to afford this place. She could cope with all sorts of disasters, she had decided, as long as she had a place to put her things.

It was Sunday and Raj had come early, bringing a gnome of a carpenter he had found in the timber section of the market, and Simrit had watched while they measured the length of one wall and discussed designs for book-shelves, decided on the wood and settled the price. The books and many of her possessions still lay unopened in crates on the floor of the room. She had panicked when all the luggage had come that morning, and had gone next door to phone

Raj, and he had arrived with the carpenter.

"Is he going to do a good job, do you think?" she had asked doubtfully.

In the life she had lived till lately she had walked into furnished accommodation, with crockery, cutlery and linen provided.

"It's his trade. We'll get the best performance out of him we can. Anyway, it's your own very first bookcase, starting from the wood. How about that? How close have you ever been to plain sawn wood before?"

"I'm not a hothouse plant," said Simrit.

He had a way of needling her to retort with his infuriating assumption that she had not really *lived*. Living, according to him, was acquaintance with things in the raw, with wood before it became furniture for instance, and with human beings at all levels—the cook or the postman as much as your husband or your grandmother. Her own ideas about life were quite different. The human element was there, of course. There were the children—the concrete, demanding details of their upbringing, and all that she gave them otherwise of herself. But there her concern with her fellow man ended. Her own replenishment came from another source, from untouched unspoilt non-human things. Explaining it to Raj she quoted a passage she had memorized as a child: "The feeling of almost physical delight in the touch of the mother-soil, of the winds that blow from Indian seas, of the rivers that stream from Indian hills..."

"Aurobindo Ghosh wrote that," she told Raj.

He was not impressed. "A writer," he insisted, "has to be concerned with people."

"I'm not that kind of writer. And I hate this century— except for the freedom it's brought for countries and people, especially for women. But it is barbaric otherwise, full of rotten, elastic standards and the worship of money. I hate the whole mess of human affairs. The only clean, clear things left are the hills and rivers and the shape of a leaf, things like that."

It had been dark since six and winter was well in, too cold to sit on the balcony after dinner, and the drawing room was full of children and unpacked luggage. There was nowhere to sit but her bedroom. She sat on the bed leaning uncomfortably against the wall, and Raj in the chair.

"Your sacred Ganges isn't very clean," he pointed out, ignoring the rest.

Simrit sat up, her face eager.

"But mountain rivers are. There's one that's absolutely unbelievable, the Beas. I got acquainted with it when Som and I drove to Kulu from Delhi some years ago. It runs alongside a motor road overhung with cliffs that almost touch the top of your car, they're so low. You feel they're going to lean over and crush you quite casually any minute. It makes a breathtaking drive. And there's this river, showing off all the way, the most ecstatic length of water you can imagine, tumbling along over rocks and boulders."

"Doesn't it ever get hold of you," she went on, "how marvellous this country is—its sheer staggering size and variety?"

She had been planning a book about India in terms of the look and texture of earth and sky—and in between all the nuances of its seasons. People wrote historical romances but here was romantic geography, almost too much for one country's share. In the far north the sixty-million-year-old Himalayas still growing, flung up from a vanished sea. Far south and three quarters of the way round, the immensity of the Indian Ocean. In between the rivers of history, the Ganges and the Brahmaputra travelling across a thousand mile plain; and then the plains themselves studded with contrasts: months of rain in tropical jungle along with sun-maddened desert. There was the way spring came to the hills with its delicate pastel display of almond blossom, tulips, narcissi and bluebells, its startling autumn fanfare of poppy and saffron, and all year round forests of blue pine and fir a day's walk from the snowline. Someone had to describe the rocky altitudes whose springs unfrozen by the thaw fell like streamers down steep slopes. It was a great objective inheritance, unbegun and unending with its cycles of steady passionless renewal. Culture came afterwards. This peninsula stretching endless miles was its source. Someone had to turn it into language.

Raj said, "This drive along the Beas, you shared it with Som, didn't you?"

"Oh God no. I sat in the car with him, that was all."

She slumped back, her animation gone.

Raj lit a cigarette.

"One of these days," said Simrit, "you're going to die of cancer."

"We're all going to die of something one of these days— those of us who aren't as good as dead already," Raj said looking steadily at her.

She was coldly angry.

"I don't know what you're trying to say."

"I'm trying to get you away from your abstractions into some kind—any kind—of life."

Why? he wondered. Why did it matter how one particular person reacted—except that in a compelling way, if this nation were ever to come to life, the educated and privileged like her must make the most, not the least, of what they had. They must magnify and expand their gifts. He was utterly convinced of that.

"What do you want out of your life, Simrit?"

"Permanence," she said promptly.

"That's not a goal. It's a hankering, because of your divorce."

"No, it's what I've always longed for. I've wanted everything to be the same forever, furniture never moved from its place, a never changing address, children growing older in the same house, a godown where tons of things could collect and not be in anybody's way, and not lose prestige, you know just because they're a bit battered and old—and where one could find them years later: toys and souvenirs and old report cards and that sort of thing. Life should be—continuous."

Som had had no use for old belongings. He had taken a childish pleasure in newness.

"Yes, but I'm talking of goals," said Raj. "You never had time to find out what you really wanted. You married young. Then you had all these children. Did you even want all of them?

"Well, I didn't think about it—"

"Good Lord, Simrit, weren't you there when it was happening? Weren't you ever consulted about anything? What kind of marriage did you have anyway?"

She could get lyrical about a river and a godown filled with her children's junk but there wasn't a spark to spare for anything that affected or even threatened her future. He wished he could jolt her into some response about practical matters. He had thought the divorce settlement dictated by her husband was the ultimate in outrage, inflicted on an unresisting, unsuspecting victim. But every layer of her past uncovered something equally shocking. The Hindu race!—mute, acquiescent, letting things happen to it, from a country to the mind and body of a woman. 'An educated woman at that. One who prized her learning and had a profession. Raj wanted to shake her violently. Had she ever been avid, really avid about anything at all? She simply could not go through life like this, letting other people's ambitions and actions overwhelm her. First it had been her husband. Next it could be her children. Woman for use had been the rule too long.

There were times when she looked rather like a child herself, suddenly abandoned and now waiting patiently for someone to tell her what to do. He knew she was nothing of the sort. She was basically tough, with the toughness of undivided integrity. And she was in his view exceptional for a woman. She had understood when she had to act, at least in that one crisis. No one who did not, could have moved bag and baggage from a whole past—with all those children. The very prospect was intimidating. No, she was not helpless. That was why he wanted to help her. Lame dogs rather repelled him. It was backbone he admired and somewhere under the wooden accuracy she reserved for everything but her writing and her children's needs, it was clear she had it. It would have been good to find some gaiety, too. He wondered if she had ever possessed it or whether it had died forever with her divorce from this unknown Som.

"Everything," he went on, "just happened to you. Marriage, children. What have you ever made up your mind about?"

Actually she hadn't. Not even about chair covers and curtains. Even there Som had had a veto. Not even about the servants. She had dismissed the cook twice for drunkenness and bad behaviour and Som had kept him on. Little things, she had thought at the time, nothing important, nothing to quarrel about, but building up into a frightening situation—herself a cog in a machine—with which it had become impossible to live. But Raj was wrong about the children. She had welcomed them.

Raj looked at his watch.

"I must go. But have you understood the tax implications of your divorce settlement or not?"

She had. He had spent all evening after the carpenter left, unravelling the legal language for her and showing her to her bewilderment the ways in which the document trapped and maimed her. Trapped and maimed were the words he had used and they were too mild, he said, to describe the damage. It was an arrangement that obviously saved Som taxation. But there were other ways to do that. The strange part of this document was its butchery, the last drop of blood extracted. It was revengeful. But revenge for what, she wondered.

"I'm going to get some advice on it then, and see how we can find a way out."

"There's no way out," said Simrit.

He brushed that aside. "There is always a way out."

"You don't understand," said Simrit. "Som is a man who sticks to the contract, whether it's right or wrong, human or inhuman. He'll never agree to any change."

"Then we'll have to leave Som out of this."

"Leave him out?"

"Yes," Raj said roughly, "out. This is not child's play, Simrit, this is a divorce. It's time to cut loose all those ragged ends, all the bleeding bits of the past, and get on with your life. And you can't with this hangman's noose around your neck."

"You don't understand," she repeated listlessly. "This agreement I've signed in his pound of flesh. He won't let it go."

"Why the devil did you sign it? You can read."

But they had been over that before. For someone of her intelligence she had a lot of stupidity to atone for. It was an incredibly stupid, yet profoundly natural thing to have done, to have believed to the last flicker that there would be fair play. There was nothing more to say about that part of it. But Raj was not at all sure she believed otherwise even now. An hour or two after he left she would have convinced herself all over again the document was all a mistake, that it didn't mean what it said. But short of staying on and drumming it into her for the rest of the night, there wasn't much more he could do.

"I don't know why you're taking so much trouble," she said.

He ground out his cigarette savagely.

"It's very simple. I don't like butchery. And this document you so blithely signed without reading or understanding it— I'll never know why—has let you in for slow butchery for as long as you live. Even a life sentence ends after fourteen years. Yours is till you die."

He hoped the brutality of it would anger her, wipe that benumbed and puzzled look off her face, as if this was her fate and she had to take it lying down. The power of her passivity was overwhelming at times. The document infuriated him every time he thought of it, and he had thought of little else since she had shown it to him a fortnight earlier. He felt violently angry as he got up to go. Her divorce settlement was burned into his brain. For part of every working day he had sat and studied it in his office and he knew it almost by heart. The crowning irony was its title—the Consent Terms. Consent! Suttees, he supposed, had given their consent too, after a fashion, as they climbed their husbands' funeral pyres.

"But it's my problem," Simrit was saying. "You behave as if it were yours."

Raj stood in the doorway, both hands in his pockets, considering the strange notion that poring over taxes might be a way of loving— objectively, of course— and asking himself if he would have gone to such lengths for another living soul.

"Well, men have gone to war without being directly involved with the issue. And haven't you ever known anyone who acted purely out of conviction?" he asked.

Without hope of reward, or honour, or even understanding? She had not.

"People do," he said, "and believe it or not, that's the most powerful motive there is."

Simrit got up and automatically smoothed the bedspread.

"All the same," she said, "this is getting rather heavily involved with a cause."

"It is. That's what living's all about," he said. He was thinking of something else as he added, "You don't grow up unless you're willing to break your heart over something."

He had been more willing to break it as a younger man. He had gone into the villages more often and found the contact with the countryside refreshing, and after each visit, the cobwebs less thick on his soul. It had something to do, he felt, with the integrated culture of the village, with values in daily use, however out of date they may have been in the rest of the world. I live a more bogus life now, he thought. Why do I do it? And what am I doing in it? Why haven't I the gumption to go and live somewhere in poverty and peace, teach men how to dig a well in the desert, plant a seed, do something *Christian*, he surprised some old echo in himself. He was certain he did not want to become too tied up with the search for security. It was not self-respecting.

Simrit went with him to the top of the stairs.

"Get to bed," he ordered. "Don't fuss around unpacking tonight."

"I won't."

"I'll give you a ring in the morning. Oh, you haven't a phone—"

It had become a joke.

"What about the milk? Are you managing?"

"Yes, very well. A boy delivers it from the market every morning with lots of clinking and clanking. I'm always afraid he'll break the bottles and half of it will get left on the stairs the way he swings them about. But his cheeks are so pink. I don't think he's more than fourteen."

"The fellow at the Delhi Milk Scheme Depot wouldn't have pink cheeks, I'm sure. So that's a bonus for you. What's the milk like?"

"Marvellous. Rich. I'm thinking of drinking some myself."

"Good idea. Why don't you?"

He looked at the pale face showing signs of strain and fatigue around the eyes. She stood leaning against the cold concrete of the bannister and some of the whitewash had come off on the dark green wool fringes of her shawl. There was a long scratch on the back of her hand and one of her nails was broken. He remembered the smooth perfection of her the first time he had met her and was oddly grateful for this contrast. It seemed to bridge a gulf of some kind.

He said, "I wish all women were ugly, Simrit."

"In heaven's name, why?" she smiled.

"Then their characters would show more. They would have to. No camouflaging frills."

"Am I ugly—or do you wish I were?"

He could never quite identify her fascination for him, which was only partly physical. It had something to do with impeccable quality, with culture, with things not remotely related to what passed as attraction between men and women. At the same time he missed humour in her. She was too walled in with her problems.

"You know very well what you are," he said. "But in your case it doesn't seem to have done you much damage."

He continued to stand a few steps below her, the wall and stairs exuding their grey chill, then said goodnight abruptly and went down. He had to stop a minute when he stepped outside. It was cold and brilliantly clear, the vast concourse of stars alone a great source of light. A world revealed and bathed in the light of the stars. The pure power and expanse of it spelled vision and opportunity. The world is on the threshold of immense changes, he thought. We've got to measure up to them, to be free-willed and creative, not the playthings of chance. We've got to take matters into our own hands. The tragedy of his own people seemed to lie in the fact that they did not. If the inert mass of them did not wake up to the fact that they were their own masters, the brutal and single-minded among them would.

Defence Colony Market consisted of two rows of shops facing each other across a miniature parklet enclosed in wrought iron. At this hour it was closed. Lately it had been spruced up in the Municipal Corporation's beautification drive. There was new paint on the shop fronts and the road was swept spotless. It catered to the needs of a mixed foreign and Indian clientele. Mostly those members of the diplomatic corps who lived in the colony and demanded good pork and fish, long-stemmed flowers and barbecue caterers. Delhi-grown white mushrooms had become a flourishing industry and were sold here, so was excellent Delhi cheese. Things were looking up. But Raj could not remember a time when he had not thought so, though the vast changes that had come over Delhi since his student days at St Stephen's College had begun to be taken for granted. This city, its past lost in antiquity, expanding now into suburbs, blossoming into new street lighting, fountains and parks, restaurants, shops and discotheques, bore no resemblance to the slow, sedate empty capital of his youth in which Old Delhi with its University and mosque and markets had had pride of place. No resemblance either to the sad, dark, stricken Delhi of the refugee migration just after the Partition.

There was a vigour and vulgarity about Delhi today, as there was about any process of growth and change. In a period of change faults could become virtues, quite different capacities come into demand. Men like Som obviously belonged to change. He was among those who blow by blow were lifting themselves away from their origins. In another generation or two they would be the elite. Tempered by humanity such men could be formidable instruments of progress. Without that, Raj doubted their lasting impact. Isolated forcefulness, isolated currents of energy undirected by vision or compassion, petered out, and at worst became aggression on their environment.

Raj took a taxi home. On the way he wondered what Simrit had looked like on that drive to Kulu as she caught and raptly held the lilt and gleam of the river and lifted her face to the sun.

4

The river had been with them since they had left the rest-house at Mandi. It was so eye-filling it captured her entire attention. Simrit watched the sunlight tremble and dissolve in it as the car went round each bend in the road. Som had hired the car and the three of them were in the back seat, she at the window nearer the river. The water was like broken green crystal as it vibrated along, yet she could see white rock and pebble glistening through it. Even the gravel at the bottom looked scraped and scoured a pure bone white. Mountain rivers were clean but she had never known one as enchanting, as riotous with its invitation to freedom.

She felt abusurdly happy looking at it, thinking that everyone should have one such river in his life.

Over beer at the tourist bungalow they had taken for a week, Vetter said, summing up their road talk, "So you think it succeeds."

Som landed his fist squarely onto the table. "We *make* it succeed."

A gleam came into Vetter's eyes. "I like that. Yah. We *make* it succeed. Your husband," he said to Simrit, "is the man I have been looking for. If anyone will put through our programme, he will. That I know." He turned back to Som and they began to discuss it again.

It suddenly struck Simrit as odd that they had come to Kulu for a week right in the middle of an ordinary April, complete with new fishing rods and camping gear. It was not holiday time. There was plenty that needed looking after in Delhi. And in any case they had never taken a holiday like this. This was a European's idea of a holiday. She and Som always went to a hotel, to efficient service and hot and cold running water. Som liked his comforts.

"Vetter was keen on it," he told Simrit when they were in their room. "He likes to fish."

"Do you like to fish?" she asked.

"Of course. You don't know your husband, do you?"

"What a pity we didn't bring Lalli. He would have enjoyed it."

Not bringing him left a ringing silence of which she was aware every minute. Since they had known Lalli hardly a day had passed without their meeting.

Som said, "Vetter and I wouldn't have had a chance to talk. Lalli is rather overwhelming. By the way Sim, I don't want you to repeat any of the discussion Vetter and I had."

"To Lalli?"

"To anybody," he said impatiently, "and naturally not to Lalli either. This is between Vetter and me. Are you coming out with us this morning?"

She decided to go. She found a place to sit on the bank where the sun sieved warmth and light through the dense cold shade of deodars. Somewhere nearby apple trees were beginning to blossom. She could smell them. There were other faint scents she could not identify. A breeze ruffled her hair and she luxuriated in her planless day. She could hear the two men further upstream, accentuating the quiet with an occasional remark. Their low measured phrases of conversation more than anything else registered Lalli's absence. This association was in a different key. They took the trout back for lunch. Vetter standing on the verandah, hands on his hips, gazing out into the fir forest, gave a big contented sigh.

"Yah. This is some scenery. Your husband knows these mountains very well."

She and Som had never been here before, but perhaps Som had been here before he married her.

"I would like to see Kashmir," Vetter went on. "He is suggesting we next do a fishing holiday in Kashmir. He says there are more varieties of trout there. Your husband is a mine of information. Fascinating. That is often the case with men who must make their own way. Self-made men. I admire this quality. What a struggle your husband must have had. Lost everything in Partition."

He was looking at her for confirmation.

"He's very—determined," said Simrit.

"Yes, yes. It is a quality I admire. We in Europe admire this very much."

After lunch the men went off together for the afternoon. When they came back they were still talking steadily, mapping out the details of an enterprise. Waking from her nap she heard them take chairs from the verandah onto the grass and sit beneath her window talking without pause.

At night she asked Som, "Are we going to do a fishing holiday with Vetter in Kashmir?"

"Yes. He wants to see something of the country and he's dead keen on fishing. We'll do it this summer."

"Weren't we planning a holiday with Lalli in the summer?"

"Nothing definite. Anyway this is more important. You have no idea how much I've got sorted out with Vetter this trip."

Som stood at the window in his pajamas, enjoying the cold crisp night air on his back. There was a subdued exultation about him that kept escaping through his voice.

"You can't begin to imagine the possibilities, Sim. What I'm doing now is chicken feed. It's next to nothing compared with what Vetter's offering me. Of course it's early days yet but with a man like Vetter and his organization—it spreads all over Europe and America—I get into international business, and then there's no further to go. I'll have made it. I'll be right on top."

The light was too dim for him to do much more than glance through the folder of notes he and Vetter had prepared. But there they were, proof positive that the kingdom of heaven was at hand. She could feel the fever in him to his fingertips, and then the swift change as he looked up. She was undressing, her pregnancy well advanced.

"The journey didn't tire you too much, did it?"

The shadow of hesitation in his eyes and voice as he left his world and waited to enter hers, touched a responsive chord in her.

"No, I slept this afternoon."

"You're sure you're all right?" He lowered himself carefully beside her on her bed. "Think this bed will hold us both? Tell me if you get tired."

But immediately the night centered exquisitely on anticipation of his next move and his next, and all that she hoped for was happening.

"Sim," he said afterward, leaving her bed, "we won't have any more children. We've got enough."

The silence stretched featureless around the rest-house except for the sound of the rushing river. She was spent and rested. Perhaps after all, she thought sleepily, there would be something in his kingdom for him and her together, something apart from the web they had spun of children and ambition. But at night she dreamt the incredible cliffs were leaning lower and lower over their car, preparing casually to crush it.

5

Simrit was dreaming, with the frightening clarity dreams
had had since her divorce. She was clinging to a balustrade
at the very top of the building, within reach of the sky, when
her fingers were wrenched loose, one by one, and she was
hurled to the pavement below. The queer thing was that
no one took any notice of her fall. Cars and people kept
going by. A deafening scream, her own, went on and on.
She could hardly hear the traffic through it. But no one
else had heard it. A man selling slices of watermelon at the
corner, crisp pink crescents, fat with juice, looked indifferently
at her and away again. Two men sitting on the ground near

her, their legs poked forward in the listless waking sleep of poverty, talked in monotonous murmurs as if no screaming casualty lay a stone's throw from them.

She closed her mouth and the noise stopped. At once pain, stupefying and deliberate, moved into her, like a live creature that had followed her body's fall. Now it invaded her as a storm comes through open windows, taking possession, fogging and muddling her, furiously upturning nerve and fibre. When it cleared she knew every bone in her body was shattered, each in splinters, every nerve laid raw. Inside her smooth unscarred skin she was all in pieces. She picked herself up in panic and was relieved to find she did not fall apart. She held. She took a deep breath. Well naturally, she reasoned. My skin is whole, not even a break or a split in it anywhere. It's the inside that has gone to pieces, and I'll just have to go along very carefully from now on. Go along very carefully, she cajoled.

The pain, a leper-like thing, detached itself from her and walked beside her to the end of the pavement, the end of the road and beyond. Every time they passed a lane or came to a crossing she prayed it would turn off by itself. But it didn't. She could see out of the corner of her eye it was still with her. She was exhausted but she dared not stop.

At sundown they came to a field dense with the dusty gold and brown of ripe grain. Across it earth and sky merged in a horizon of exquisite, unbearable beauty, restless with colour. This lovely earth, thought Simrit catching her breath, this lovely, lovely earth, and everything that's in it. She could turn then to look at the pain. She was meant, she knew, to accept it peacefully, without reason or question. There was nothing else to be done. A person thrown out of a train in the night and forced to find his way home in the dark must feel like this.

Simrit woke with a start to the familiar sound of the milk bottles and saw from her bedside clock that it was just six and pitch dark. It was part of her cautious daily ritual to wait when she woke for the pain to catch up with her. She tried to anticipate the form it would take today. Sometimes it caught at her ribs or her throat, or scalded her stomach like bile thrown off course. Or it could come as a creeping lethargy of the limbs, draining her of will and energy. That was the worst, with the day unrolling dully before her, cutting her off hour after hour from the rest of the world, from remembered sights and sounds — a kettle on the boil, the clink of teacups, a segment of sunlit garden, a room comfortingly familiar seen through one's mirror.

There was another ritual through which she tried to trace how she could have behaved differently, how averted the calamitous event. But there were moments in life when one was impelled by an absolute conviction greater than right or wrong, and then one burned at the stake if need be.

On most days she was fully awake as soon as she opened her eyes, another effect of the divorce. It had flung her into a twenty-four hour alertness of which even her dreams seemed an inseparable part. It reminded her now that at half-past nine Moolchand, Som's company lawyer, was coming to see her at her request. Raj had not seen much point in her talking to him. But it was just possible, she had insisted, there was a mistake or a misunderstanding in the Consent Terms that a friendly meeting could rectify. The thought was consoling as she got out of bed, went into the bathroom and switched on the light and the hot water geyser. Electric daylight flooded the room and her dark fancies dissolved. There must be a mistake, she told herself. No one treats another person like that, even when forgiveness is impossible. She stared at her wide-awake face in the mirror. Som could have forgiven her if she had been a weaker being, unsure, dependent, even deceiving. But that beneath her docility she was none of these things was unpardonable. And she could have loved him in spite of everything, if only sometimes she had fought him.

At exactly nine-thirty Moolchand came past the dining table scattered with toast crumbs and the remains of fried eggs. He made his way between crates and boxes and sat down, avoiding the sharp nails and jagged edges of those that had been pried open. He withdrew a pink file cover from his brief-case and placed it squarely on his knees. The sun reflected through the glass doors of the drawing room touched his black patent leather shoes with a satin shine and danced on the blue-green cut-glass ashtray Simrit had put on the table near him. Moolchand did not smoke. Simrit had put it there as a talisman, hoping it would bring her luck. It was solid as crystal, yet it had a rim curling with the miraculous delicacy of petals. She had not been able to resist buying it at the Kerala Handicrafts Emporium. It had cost thirty rupees, an extravagance she could no longer afford. I must stop thinking about money, she instructed herself.

"Now what is the problem, Mrs Raman?"

The problem. The enormity of the problem flooded her. She wanted to rant and rave, pierce him somehow with her necessity. Or should she force herself to be brief and precise and state only the crux of the matter like: "I've been in an earthquake, Mr Moolchand, and every single thing I knew is rubble around me. That's the problem." Or "The problem, Mr Moolchand, is that I have been pushed off a fifty-storey building and every bone in my body is broken."

53

But surely he knew what the problem was? It was he who had drafted the Consent Terms.

She had never said much more than "Have some more ice cream" to Moolchand at office parties. She knew nothing whatever about him. They had circulated in each other's orbit without ever really looking at each other. She noticed now that he was jowly and light-skinned with a small girlish mouth. The kind of man who would take sweets out of his pocket for children and, she puzzled, draw up terms like the ones he had. Only of course he had done as he was told. So had she, after all, until nearly the very end. Didn't that give them something in common? The wild improbability of her situation struck her afresh. Why was she sitting in a room in Defence Colony surrounded by luggage, with Moolchand opposite—Moolchand, scarcely known, who had suddenly become the arbiter of her fate? None of it was really happening, so there was nothing to say.

Moolchand waited, imperturbable and polite, not reminding her he would be late for office, and Simrit realized she had not said a word. She wanted to put the point very clearly.

Moolchand suddenly began, "I want to tell you how sad I consider all this...so unbelievable...all my sympathies ...the children...anything I can do..."

As if someone had died. Well, well, nobody was dead yet. It was a bracing thought.

"I'm sorry to have kept you away from office — " Simrit began, pleasant and businesslike.

Now that she had begun to talk all she felt was a terrible matter-of-factness in which her voice had somehow gained the tone and timbre her feelings had lost. She was quite astonished at the sound of her own voice, and it spurred her efficiently on.

Moolchand waved her apology away.

" — but I did want to talk to you about the terms of the settlement," she went on.

The terms, now that she understood them, left a bad taste in her mouth. She wanted to have nothing to do with this settlement.

"I have the document here," Moolchand patted the pink file.

"I've discovered—and it came as quite a shock to me—it leaves me in a very bad position."

Moolchand sat expressionless.

"I'm not complaining about the support, though heaven knows it's little enough," said Simrit smoothly. "I'll manage somehow, provided I am free to earn. It's the amount of tax I'll have to pay because all those shares, six lakhs' worth, belonging to Mr Raman are in my name. After all, he controls them and I get nothing out of them, yet the tax on them will wipe out all my own earnings."

"It is a substantial body of shares," Moolchand reverentially agreed, missing the point. "Not the sort one can build up any more with the economic policy of the Government as unpredictable as it is."

"I understand that," said Simrit. "It's just that I don't want them in my name. I get nothing out of them. So why should I be taxed at an exorbitant rate because of them?"

Moolchand spoke earnestly. "That body of shares, Mrs Raman, goes, as you know, eventually to your son."

"Not until he's twenty-five — nine years from now — " said Simrit, "and meanwhile I have to pay these huge taxes."

She was beginning, she felt, to sound like a cracked record with the needle stuck in the crack. Besides, Mr

Moolchand, she wanted to add, no one should *have* that kind of money with no effort, certainly not just one child out of so many children.

"Mr Raman wisely decided the boy should inherit when he is mature, knowing the temptations of money for the young."

Not to mention their elders, said Simrit silently. She tried to imagine Moolchand untempted by money. The picture was very indistinct. Som ignoring money wasn't there at all. But she was making no headway with Moolchand.

"Yes, all right, if that's how he wants it. But I don't want the shares left in my name. As long as they are, I'll have to pay this crippling tax and whatever I earn will just be wiped out by the tax, don't you see?"

I suppose, she thought, this is what an overloaded donkey feels like standing there as large as life with its back breaking, and no one doing anything about it, not because they can't see it, but because it's a donkey and loads are for donkeys.

"A lady like you — having to earn — " Moolchand shook his head in disbelief.

Simrit interrupted him, "Why can't it be made into a trust for my son? Isn't that what people do with large sums of money?"

"Because, Mrs Raman, there would be a big gifts tax if we made a trust."

"Well it would be paid once and that would be the end of the misery. This way—"

"Mrs Raman," said Moolchand with patience, "no one sees a sum like that nowadays. To dissipate it by incurring gifts tax would be unthinkable."

"Then why can't Mr Raman pay the extra tax on it himself?"

Moolchand looked as if he was in possession of some higher truth which he had to explain very simply to an idiot child.

With infinite kindness he said, "Because added to what Mr Raman already pays on his salary, the tax would be extortionate. Unthinkable." He thought it over and repeated "Unthinkable."

Apparently the only thinkable thought was the guillotine for her. The meat grinder. Moolchand, she remembered irrelevantly, was a vegetarian. They didn't eat flesh but they could slaughter their own kind, under instructions of course, and on payment.

"I see," she said dryly. "So I have to be the pack animal."

"Now, Mrs Raman —"

Maybe she had always been an animal, only a nice, obedient, domestic one, sitting on a cushion, doing as she was told. And in return she had been fed and sheltered. Now she mustn't whine if they threw stones at her, or even a killing boulder like the Consent Terms. Simrit collected herself. She must, *must* get Moolchand to understand. He would understand figures. He dealt in them. He would grasp the horror of it at once. It had just not struck him.

She said, "Look Mr Moolchand, this is the way the agreement works out in actual figures."

She fetched paper and pencil and wrote them down for him. The columns rose up grim and separate, each proclaiming its damage to her, devastating whatever effort she might make to earn and save.

At the end Moolchand said, with a hint of displeasure, "I can convey your sentiments to Mr Raman if you wish."

"Yes," she said, "I do wish it."

She held out the paper she had been writing on.

57

"That won't be necessary," he said. "I have understood your argument."

My argument? The argument. This was a question of fundamentals. Would Som have let anyone do this to him? And Raj had said no court in any other part of the civilized world have allowed it. She folded the piece of paper over and over until it was a hard little knob in the palm of her hand. She was unnerved by Moolchand's indifference and her composure momentarily deserted her.

"I have to bring up my children," she said distractedly. "Even my son—before he inherits these holy hoarded lakhs—has to have his school bills and all his other bills paid. And you have no idea the amount children eat. And what a lot of shoes they need."

"You wished yourself to have the children in your custody," Moolchand pointed out.

"Of course, I did," she cried irrationally, "they're mine."

She had taken away with her as much as she could of the marriage all in one piece, all the living wealth of it, and had left behind the crockery and furniture and linen and jewels and silver. And now, she thought miserably, I've got nothing to give the children except myself, and is that going to be enough? Som's got all the things, the cars, the bank accounts, the whole circus.

Moolchand watching her must have realized he was on different, shaky ground.

He said, "Mr Raman would be glad to have the children. But unconditionally, of course. With him they would want for nothing."

"No of course not. There would be cars and the house and trips and lots more pocket money," she intoned.

"Yes, yes," he asserted.

"That's what I thought," said Simrit, her face hard.

Moolchand ran his finger along the edge of the file. He cleared his throat.

"Mr Raman's concern is for the corpus—this body of shares. The corpus should remain unharmed. We hope, with care, to swell it considerably, oh considerably, before the boy comes into his inheritance."

And the taxes with it. The corpus, a fat, hideous, bloated monster, swelling fit to burst, crowded her imagination. The dynosaurs at least had died of their size. This monstrosity would feed and thrive—on her.

"This is a charming flat," Moolchand was remarking.

"It costs seven hundred and fifty a month," she said levelly, "and we're crammed into it like sardines. And even if I do manage to earn more, it will all go into paying tax on account of the—the corpus."

Moolchand looked sad and immovable. A cool customer, he must think her, with all the figures at her fingertips. Simrit, matter-of-fact in her anxiety to display no emotion, knew it was the wrong approach. And she could make no other. A life lived bringing up children and writing books did not teach one how to be an actress. One was as one was. Moolchand might have reacted better if she had broken down and wept, pleaded her plight, not displayed this control and competence. She was something outside his experience, a woman who exercised her mind.

He said, suddenly faceless as though delivering a sentence, "This is not a private arrangement between you and Mr Raman. The Consent Terms are law."

She wanted to burst out that there were people behind the law, that people made the law and could change it. The law was not an enemy. But she sat stock still, the little knob of paper in her hand. She realized how desperately she had been waiting for a sign from Moolchand that the terms could be altered, made just and fair. And the most paralyzing revelation in the whole nightmare was that it was not a mistake, not an arrangement set down in anger that could be rectified now with good-will. It was *intended* that she should carry the burden of the highest rates of tax. Taxes were not a field where Som made mistakes. These, then, were his ethics. I can no longer say it couldn't be true, she thought. It *is* true. Even a blind creature, even *I* know that now. She felt surrounded by a remorseless, complicated machinery from which there was no escape, all because of money. She wondered why she had not seen it before. Money had been part of the texture of her relationship with Som, an emotional, forceful ingredient of it, intimately tied to his self-esteem. Money was, after all, a form of pride, even of violence. Still this discovery was sinister and unnatural, like watching a tide creep in the wrong direction.

"I must remind you, Mrs Raman," Moolchand continued in the same formal vein, "that this was a negotiated settlement to which you gave your consent."

Something in her ripped and tore with the finality of it. What a lie the facts could be, what an appalling lie. Nothing, almost *nothing* was ever negotiated. Negotiation was a myth—except among equals—and where on this earth did equals exist? The side with the bargaining power called the tune, while the other signed on the dotted line. That was what Raj had said and he was right. Suddenly she ached for Raj, for the clean untainted atmosphere he carried with him.

"Will there be any other message for Mr Raman?" asked Moolchand.

Mr Raman. Mr Raman. Why couldn't Som talk to her himself? But she knew he would not. It was easier to think of her as an enemy in the path he had set for himself

She looked at the ashtray, the colour of dazzling moulded water. Here and there it had flaws where bubbles had formed in the glass. Her little talisman had not worked after all.

Moolchand rose.

"If you will permit, I must get to my office."

Simrit got up with him.

"Mind the stairs," she said. "That sharp turn is tricky."

It was a very different leave-taking from their last one, with Moolchand affable, vague and glowing after a party, Scotch and imported asparagus stowed away inside him behind his starched shirt front. She could not help seeing the grime in the corners of the uncarpeted stone stairs. The sweeper woman who came twice a day had a lovely face and a bell-like voice, but she wielded a careless broom. Yet Simrit could stand on those stairs with Raj, forgetting the dirt.

Up in the *barasti* room she picked up the weights her son exercised with, and rescued his chest expander from under a chair. The doors of the wall cupboard were decorated with magazine pictures of motor cars stuck on with Scotch tape. Brij shared the room with two of his sisters, but it was triumphantly his room. Young as he was he already exercised an unconscious superiority, the ancient male prerogative. Simrit looked appraisingly at the cars, trying to partake of her son's fascination for them. She could not even drive one. Machinery, except for her typewriter, had never interested her, a distinct shortcoming in a world that judged people by the machinery they kept, not the company. What mattered was the one in the garage, the kind and quantity that burred and whirred in one's kitchen, the artificial temperature a machine kept in one's bedroom. She passed on to a section of wall pasted with pictures of muscle men, the men her son thought beautiful, their diaphragms caving in to show powerful chests, arm muscles ballooning out.

She went out onto the terrace. It was open to the sky — useful for summer entertaining, the landlord, a nice, ex-military type, had said. She had not pointed out that in summer the barsati room, so full of welcome sun now, would be a furnace. She had not thought as far ahead as the summer.

A clean clamouring grass smell came up from the garden below. She turned to find her son behind her, holding a slim twisted bough of red rose creeper. Simrit thought of him as "her son" and her eldest girl as "her daughter," and all the rest as "the children," because they had not yet confronted her with their nearly final personalities and still counted as part of her own body warmth. These two stood apart from it, very individual, half adult, somewhat strangers, for whom her concern was deep and separate, and not an extension of all that she felt and needed for herself.

"I brought this for your desk, Mama."

Together they looked down at the rose creeper entwining the garden wall of the ground floor tenant, and then at each other.

"It's from there, isn't it?" she asked.

Brij shrugged.

"Oh darling, you shouldn't have. They're his."

"That's all right, Mama. What are you worried about? I'll beat him up if he says anything," said her son tranquilly, snaking the muscle in his sturdy right arm.

"No, don't do anything of the sort," she said hastily. "There's no need for it."

Whatever had happened to non-violence, to not touching other people's property, to the meek inheriting the earth?

"I beat up Ronnie Malhotra last term in school. I gave him a thrashing he'll never forget."

"Oh, poor fellow, why?"

"He said something I didn't like, something stupid. Anyway I taught him a lesson."

When you built up muscles like that, thought Simrit, you had to use them on someone. And was it his fault if in all these thousands of years of life on this planet, no one had made peace as heroic as war? She looked at the youth and strength of the boy beside her and longed to touch his consciousness with something different, some true and everlasting thing. A thing never to be possessed, only to be loved and served. How few dreams these young had, with everything known and experienced and conquered.

"Wasn't that Mr Moolchand from Papa's office who was here? I saw him leave a little while ago. He waved as he was getting into his car. What a car!"

"His car? I didn't notice it."

"What did he come here for?"

"I asked him to come. I wanted to talk to him about the terms of the financial agreement between Papa and me."

Brij had taken a length of twine from his pocket and was winding it round his wrist. She wanted to explain the terms to him and to do it neutrally, if one could be neutral about crimes.

"He wasn't much help," she said, "but perhaps Papa will work out some way that will put less of a burden on me."

She waited for him to say something. He was playing with his twine.

"I want to go and see Papa," he said after a pause. "He said to drop in whenever I liked."

Simrit felt strangely helpless.

"Yes you should."

She must talk to Brij, but how did one begin to explain a document like that? Not that she wanted to preserve a particular image of his father. The facts were more important. Nor did she want to defend a crime. That would be beyond her power to do. What mattered was to protect both their characters, her son's and her own, from curdling.

"Do you need me for anything?" he asked.

"No, I'm going to try and get my room in order."

"Then I'm going out to buy some film for my camera. I might look in on Papa at his office later."

It was painful how the connection continued, like a detached heartbeat. The tissue of a marriage could be dissolved by human acts, but its anatomy went on and on. And skeletons could endure for a million years. Just living together, daily routine produced that uncanny durability. It made the question of whether one had loved or not, been loved or not, been the transgressor or transgressed against, trivial by comparison. For her the connection continued through the children, for Som perhaps even through the furniture. Unless, being Som, he had thrown it all out and started afresh with another lot. The way he did with his clothes by the armful, with letters and remembrances and even with friends. A new set to go with a new phase of existence, as if the past were soaked in a guilt whose every vestige he had sworn to wipe out. Som did not have a multiple self to cope with. He did not agonize over possibilities. He was just what he was at the moment. No past, not even its crumbs, no manure as it were, for anything else to begin growing in. She wondered how he destroyed his memories. Did he nail them down in coffins and let them pulsate there till they rotted?

Simrit went downstairs to the little enclosure she had made

into a room for her daughter. It was a litter of clothes, re-cords and magazines. She picked up a magazine lying open on the bed. It was full of advertisements picturing lavishly beautiful young people with long bare limbs and shining hair. Simrit found the page of contents. One short story, a couple of articles, two columns about books, another about theatre and films, and the rest, page upon page of induce-ment to buy. Shopping could evidently become a whole-time job, a seasonal cycle of frenzied feminine activity. She sat down on the rumpled bed and glanced through one of the articles. It was about the women of a famous millionaire family and where they did their shopping, from country to country, autumn and spring, summer and winter, apparent-ly all their lives. It was a life that made sense, too, to Som and Lalli, to Vetter and the man from Leeds, all the people who for years had moved through her world. And now to her daughter.

The window framed a dipping branch weighted with leaf and white star-shaped blossom. Only the little children had spoken of it. The older ones had not even noticed it, and yet her daughter lay on this bed and saw it on waking every morning.

6

Each time Brij entered his father's office, something delicious happened to him. Everything about the office was controlled and immaculate. The temperature for one thing. Whatever it was like outside, here the air was exactly right. The sounds were subdued office sounds. In the main room where the secretaries and stenographers sat with frosted glass partitions between them, typewriters discreetly punctuated the silence. There were brand new journals on technology and engineering symmetrically placed on a round table in the visitors' section of the room. Not a scratch or a smudge on any glossy wood or glass surface. The chairs were upholstered in moss green leather framed in dark teak. There was a coffee-coloured pile carpet. Brij breathed deeply. It was beautiful.

The red light on his father's door meant there was someone in there with him and he was not to be disturbed. But Mrs Farrow had instructions that Brij could go in any time. He was in no hurry. He loved to sit here taking it all in, but Mrs Farrow had seen him from her desk in its privileged corner. She waved and he went up to say hello.

"So, how's life, Brij?"

"Fine."

Mrs Farrow gave him chocolates, arranged movie tickets for him and his friends, had taken him to the dentist when Mama had had to be away somewhere, and home to tea occasionally. She was jolly and kind.

"You should come and see us more often."

"I'm going to. I've been busy helping Mama get the flat settled."

"What's it like?"

"It's all right."

He was not bothered about the flat. He would be in it less than a month longer, until his winter vacation came to an end, then back to school till summer, and again till the end of the year. That would be the end of school, and excitement took hold of him when he thought of what might happen afterwards. Papa was always talking about it, not promising anything but dangling a hope.

"You want to see your Pa? You can go in."

"In" was even better, much better than the main room. The gorgeous purple silk handloomed curtains, the enormous expanse of gleaming rosewood desk with its two different coloured telephones, the wall behind it entirely panelled and two elaborate wooden friezes that looked odd to Brij but which Mrs Farrow had told him cost his Pa a packet at the antique dealers in Sundar Nagar. The mere touch of that bell on the desk brought instant response. The room enshrined authority and money, the things Brij knew spelled safety. The sights and sounds that made for discomfort and disturbance couldn't touch it. Through those glass windows three floors up from street level one could have been anywhere, not in Delhi. Winter abroad must look like that, thought Brij, looking down on leafless branches and yellow-brown leaves scattered and squashed at intervals on the pavement. Abroad was where Brij wanted badly to go, where he *would* go if Pa approved of him, if he did well enough.

"Well, come along, Brij," said his father. "You can tell it all to him now, Moolchand," he said to the man opposite him, "now that he's here in person."

Brij noticed the cut of his father's suit, the red shirt, the broad tie—the styles they were wearing abroad. The glow of confidence about his father entered into him. He sat down feeling different, bigger, taller, successful. As if he'd come here in a Mercedes instead of on his bicycle.

Moolchand had a company of his own, besides advising Pa's company on legal matters, but even he spoke in an altered tone in Pa's presence. Pa seemed to have that effect on people, make them shrink and shrivel. He had had it on Brij at one time, when he had been much younger, nine, ten years old and had run to hide to escape his father's temper, the angry roar of disapproval that had so terrified him. He had run to the godown, trying to feel safe among the boxes, hidden his face in the folds of his mother's sari— anywhere to get away. Stupid of him, he thought now. The roar had after all been only a loud voice. He could face up to it now and a lot else besides. I suppose it's because I've come to know him, he thought in surprise, wondering if other people had to get to know their fathers, or whether they knew them from the start. He had never had such a thought about his mother. He always seemed to have known her. Knowledge of Pa had been gradual, hammered in by specific incidents, buttressed by "if." That was how Brij had described it to himself and to his friends. "You'll get that gun if—," "I'll give you a hundered rupees if—." If he did well in his exams. If he got his swimming or his boxing blue. If he built up his muscles. If. "You don't get something for nothing," his father had said and all along it had been Prove Yourself. Be tough. Be a winner. Be a man, The kind of man who batters his way through opposition— and arrives. Like his father. Yes, now he understood his father and wanted quite desperately to measure up to his standards, to wear clothes like him, one day to sit behind that desk and give orders like him. Brij's admiration was genuine and wholehearted. What made him uneasy was the definite distance between him and Pa, the little journey to be made each time to acceptance, to the moment of complete security when the sound of that longed-for voice and laugh told Brij all was well and that he, today, was on sure ground.

"Go on," said his father to Moolchand, "explain it to him. He's old enough to know what he's going to inherit."

Brij took the chair near Moolchand, placed his arms along the chair arms, then lowered them and rested his hands on his knees. His muscle building had given him a solidity and bulk unusual for his age, so that he felt more comfortable on the playing field than in a chair, and sitting still for any length of time was not in any case easy for him. He finally decided to keep one arm on the chair arm and the other down beside him on the seat.

He cleared his throat to be certain of his voice and asked,

"What's this about, Pa?"

"Moolchand will explain. It's about the money you're going to inherit. It's all there in the agreement between me and your mother."

Brij felt a constriction in his throat he could not dispel by swallowing. For three miles on his bicycle he had banished the thought, to be greeted by it here. He listened warily to Moolchand. Five lakhs, he heard, was coming to him, the rest to be divided among his sisters. It was six lakhs now, that is, but it would grow. It was all invested in his father's own company. Profits this year had been one hundred per cent. His father and Moolchand discussed figures for a bit, and cracked a joke Brij did not understand.

"Your're going to be a millionaire, boy," said Pa.

The word dazed Brij and sent a flush to his face. He was suddenly grappling with a flurry of emotion. He didn't know if he was going to laugh or cry. He sat stock still praying he would do neither.

"Well, how do you feel about that?" asked his father.

Brij cleared his throat and spoke but his voice got left behind and Moolchand and his father laughed heartily. His father went on laughing, slapping the table with his hand and soon Brij was laughing with him. Man to man. It was like a swift and joyful reunion, this comradeship of laughter. I love my father when he laughs, I love him. He and his father were on top of the world, far above the workaday mass of ordinary mortals, far above anything and anyone. His father had made it to the millions and he was going to get them from him and double them and treble them. Brij turned the feel of lakhs over on his tongue. Here he was sitting in Pa's office listening to lakhs! His own thrilling lakhs!

Moolchand was telling Pa that his mother wanted that

money taken out of her name. Only, to do it would incur a gifts tax of about two lakhs. His father was retorting that no one in his senses would want to lose two lakhs, money that would eventually go to the children. That was a lot of money to pay in gifts tax to the bloody Government. So of course it must remain in his mother's name until it came to him. Fragments of conversation Brij had heard that morning between his mother and Moolchand connected in his mind. Why couldn't the Company pay the extra taxes, he wondered. Why couldn't Pa? The words formed in his mind. He rehearsed them carefully while Pa and Moolchand talked: "Pa, I was thinking, couldn't it be worked out so that you could pay the extra taxes —" No, not so blunt, though Pa might like it that he had understood the finance of it. "Pa, what I was thinking was that—" Was what? He felt a little feverish trying to think of the right way to say it, the way that wouldn't upset Pa, would keep him friendly. But it was too big a risk. He didn't dare.

His father took a cigar from the carved sandalwood box lined with green felt on his desk, and offered one to Moolchand. Brij watched the ritual of lighting it. The tip was cut off with a special slicer and a long match, special for cigars, turned the flame just below the tip, evenly, expertly. Everything around Pa was special, exclusive, made to order. The heavy sweetish aroma filled the room, adding somehow to the aura of security. The sharp nagging little pain that had started in Brij got stoppered up with it. It goaded him savagely sometimes, not often, and not always noticeably. Or it was like a leak and he plugged it, stopped it at once by thinking of something else — like Raquel Welch in her last movie, or the way his best friend Rishad had performed so terrifically in the last school swimming meet, those great long windmill arms of his cutting the water like knives. He didn't need to think of anything now with the cigar smoke rich and thickly protective invading his nostrils. As a little boy it had made him feel physically sick. Like the sight of beggars. He had screamed once when a beggar's sore-covered hand had reached into the car for alms. "The boy's a sissy," his father had said disgustedly. But he had outgrown all that and become tough. Somewhere at the bottom of his mind lingered a sentence, entangled in memory with the shine and shade of a calm day, a holiday, a time of story-telling, and his mother saying: "There are two kinds of strength, you know, Brij, the physical kind we can see and the invisible inner kind." But that had been a story. In life there was only one kind, the battling kind.

"Well, do you understand the settlement?" his father asked.

Brij nodded. He didn't—exactly. The bit about his mother was worrying him. The words he hadn't said remained darkly inside him, adding themselves to a growing feeling of acute discomfort. He plugged it determinedly.

"Good. The principal will be kept in trust till you're twenty-five. But long before that, as soon as you finish your education, you'll have a substantial income from it. Until then it will remain in your mother's name."

The crowded Defence Colony flat came back to him, his things all jumbled up with the girls', Mama coping with it. And now these taxes. . . . But I will look after her, he decided. I'll do so much for her. I won't let anything hurt her. When I'm older I'll help her out. He stopped the dark thoughts. Stupid people weren't happy because they didn't realize that life had to be lived in compartments. Father in one, mother in another. Two lives, not one, with loyalty to each carefully apportioned, nothing lost—which those ninny sisters of his didn't seem to realize. Of course they weren't in his position. Pa was explaining about the lakhs, and his obligation to them, as he pressed the bell on his desk. The door opened almost at once, and he ordered a cold drink for Brij in the same tone of voice without turning to look at the man at the door. Brij knew the man and liked him. They had played marbles together on the downstairs steps when he had been a kid. He wished Pa had looked at him.

"How would you like to lunch with me at the *Rotisserie?*" said his father.

"I'd love it," he said promptly.

Brij knew what he was going to order. Steak—rare, fried potatoes and a special salad. And a huge dessert with chunks of whipped cream.

"Mr Vetter will be at lunch too. He arrived from Milan this morning. And we can ask him what he advises you should do after school."

"You mean which college?"

"Yes, abroad. If you do well enough, of course."

Brij could hardly breathe. He stifled his excitement. It was too early to get excited. If. But he would do well enough. He'd cram. He'd slave. Here it came, his chance to get away from the pain and the prickles and the very stuff out of which they all came. Another world to go away to.

He excused himself to go and wash his hands. From Mrs Farrow's desk he phoned his mother to tell her he would be lunching with his father.

"All right, darling."

He could tell from her voice that she had been busy and was far away at the moment, but it quickly changed to vibrancy.

"Remember when Pa and I took you there and you ate too much dessert and were sick afterwards?"

They laughed and chatted, recalling the incident, then Brij

73

said goodbye, put the phone down and went into the bathroom. He remembered that day clearly. It had been his first day home from boarding school and Mama and Papa had taken him out to lunch as a treat. Years ago, this was. They had teased him about the way he was stuffing himself and warned him of the consequences. And it had been a joke for a long time afterwards how gruesome he had felt after that tuck-in. Brij stared at the gleaming white enamel of the wash basin, the tears smarting his eyes, agony in his chest, and thought fiercely of Raquel Welch.

7

Simrit was at her desk, but it was a long time since she had been able to write. Even reminders of writing looked distant. In her scribble book notes stretched like untidy knitting across the pages, the pencil jottings smudgy and indistinct. She opened her file. These notes were in clear close type, but someone else in another time had laboured at them. Strange that at some time last year she had felt concentrated enough to sit down and do this work, producing page after page of description. Now the effort to write was like going against nature.

She stood the bough of rose creeper Brij had given her

in a glass of water on her desk. Still in bud, it would open tomorrow into sweet, undistinguished, ragged petals with a fuzzy gold centre. Its aristocracy lay in its stem and its pure pale green thorn, exquisitely precise and treacherous. The size and shape, the literal presence of objects had begun to be etched on her mind as the meaning between her and Som had receded, and she, never a fighter, had faded quietly out of the arena. There, beyond the known embattled pattern and routine, driven more intensely into herself, her crying sense of loss was replaced by a new attentiveness. She would go to her room, close the door, shut out the world in a grief too continuous to be catered to, and become aware of a current that made its way through life unnoticed unless one stopped and looked. The horizontal grain in the light brown wood of her desk revealed the lovely inner structure of its tree, and all around her there were familiar objects, a regular panorama of non-life to be observed and enjoyed. After a while these met some need in her, providing a contentment that busy living lacked. The *Isha Upanishad*, book of antiquity, explained it: "*The whole world is the garment of the Lord. Renounce it, then, and receive it back as the gift of God.*" The whole world, not just the living, but every particle and atom, all creation.

Som had been able to say more and more often: "Simrit can't come this evening," or "Simrit is tied up with the children to-day. She's a very good mother, you know." And later frankly non-plussed, "Simrit's not keeping well. I don't know what it is. She's just run down, probably nothing serious. She's too tired to go out." And the posse of European businessmen fresh off their jets and soon to fly again, would courteously take their leave of her to go with Som where the action was, where the grids turned. They did not discuss business in her presence any more than Lalli had.

Either business was something obscene and unmentionable, or women were morons—she wasn't sure which—so most of Som stayed cut off from her. Her usefulness to him had never extended to areas of the mind. The Europeans understood this. It fitted. Woman in the home was a good, sound idea. Europeans even had a nostalgia for it, as they had for the glamour of so many institutions they had thankfully dispensed with themselves.

She heard Som saying to Rudy Vetter in the next room, "I'm worried about Simrit. She's not herself."

"How do you mean that?" she heard Vetter interestedly enquire.

"I don't know," came the reply. "I have no idea, Rudy. I'm all at sea."

Som was standing there, she guessed, legs apart, banging one fist into the other palm, as he did when something did not obediently fit into the compartment provided for it.

"Has she had a medical check-up?"

"Yes, yes, the lot. There's absolutely nothing the matter with her physically. That's what's worrying me."

The implication, insidious as mist, of nerves, of neurosis outside the understanding of a normal, healthy man. It agitated Simrit. She felt her hands go sweaty.

"Then she has this dramatic way of putting things," she heard Som continue. "Now, I'm busy. Who isn't? I'm away a lot—it's part of the game."

She could imagine him hands widespread, palms up.

"—I can understand that upsetting a woman, but she calls it destruction." He laughed ruefully. "Oh not of our marriage. I could even understand that. She doesn't need me to spend more time with her—she's very complete with the children and her writing and the rest of it—she wants me to spend more time with *myself*. You know sit and contemplate about goals and so on."

Vetter said something Simrit did not hear.

"No, no, not literally, but—you know—think about things. Think with a capital T, and about matters not connected with what I have to do from morning till night. Tell her she's got more to give the children because of the business and the life I lead—more money, more extras—and it's just so much water off a duck's back. She just doesn't care."

"She is so very high-strung, so sensitive—" said Vetter.

"Yes, but it has come to the point where she burst into tears because I gave Brij a hundred rupees for doing well in his last term report. I tried to talk to her about it and she said why didn't I offer to teach him tennis instead, spend a little more time with him. I've fixed up the best marker at the Club to teach him."

There was, Simrit thought, an edge of enjoyment on the fringes of Som's perplexity. It was still, to him, an understandable situation. She was an object of pity and tenderness, a "poor little thing."

Vetter said she should go with Som to Germany on his next trip and get a proper checkup.

"She'll never do that," said Som. "She has become awfully touchy about that sort of suggestion, and in any case she'll never leave India for a check up. She's quite mulish about everything being just as good here."

"Well—maybe," said Vetter doubtfully. "It is just a suggestion."

"How long have we known Vetter?" Simrit asked Som after he had gone.

"Rudy? I don't know. Five, six months."

"But you never liked him—until lately. You said you didn't trust him. You said he was a go-getter."

"Did I?"

"Don't you remember? You said you wouldn't go near any business deal with him. How could you start working with him if you didn't trust him?"

"Of course I trust him. Don't be ridiculous. The deal is on and it couldn't be going better."

"Yes but before this deal you said you didn't trust him. When did you start trusting him?"

Som said evenly, "You're not yourself these days."

"I want to know how you make friends. You did say—"

Som crashed his fist down onto the table. Its heavy glass top took the blow without damage but a vase too near the edge fell on its side and water poured into the carpet. It soaked through leaving a soggy dark hole.

"What if I bloody well did? I've changed my mind."

She had always taken the violence of his gestures for granted. Why did they suddenly seem part of a total pent-up violence? His mind? Was that what had changed? Her hands were sweating again and tears were gathering in her eyes ready to spill. Som rang a bell and ordered a servant to wipe the table and take away the vase. Like a man with no inner power or authority but the emblems of both in abundance. All the iron and steel on the outside. Oh Som! She went to him and clung. It was so restful to stand there like that in the daytime, in this room, with all their clothes on and seeking no goal but tenderness. Her arms tightened around him. He held her off awkwardly after a moment.

"What have you got against Rudy?" he demanded.

"I?"

"Yes, why the inquisition?"

"But I like him," she said.

Som's association with Vetter had begun so suddenly and blossomed overnight into one of those immensely successful business collaborations graduating rapidly to blood brotherhood, that Som had such a talent for. Vetter soon became a regular visitor to their home. By that time her husband, too, was one of the men off the jets, his expensive soft leather briefcase hardly ever put down. The sparring, the jokes, the arranging and rearranging of programmes were carried on from jet to ground and back again. Somewhere in between she caught snatches of them. And there was so much laughter because business was going so fantastically well. It took possession of the house, made a carnival of arrivals and departures, setting everything in motion, the swings, the roundabouts and the giant wheel. And they seemed to go from carnival to carnival. German-accented voices sky-rocketed all over the house. The children came, irresistibly attracted, and stood curiously in doorways listening. Som would sweep one or another of them up into the air in a burst of physical well-being and the certain delight of success that oiled and tempered all his reactions.

"And what have you learned while I've been away?" he would ask.

But there was no time to wait for an answer.

And then Vetter started coming more often to India, staying with them instead of at a hotel, his familiar broad back barring the light from the drawing room window. Vetter was kind and interested. He tried to bridge the gaping void between her and Som, struggling earnestly to understand the enigma—her—for who could be easier to understand than Som, a man with a zest for food and drink, dedicated to success and what it took to get there. In fact, a man, the kind the German had never before associated with India in all his former vegetarian, teetotal business contacts. Didn't Simrit know she was the luckiest woman in the world? She could have anything she liked, clothes, jewels, anything. Why was she not *happy*?

"Why are you not *happy?*" he pleaded with her.

Yes, with all her toys, she wondered, why was she not happy?

"Som is doing all this for you," Vetter had said in his patient, persistent way.

"Don't!" she had stopped him tensely. "Don't ever say that."

Vetter had stared at her uncomprehendingly, then shrugged and got up to walk around the room and talk in his precise German English. Her glance followed the backs of his shoes, then their toes, of brown Italian suede, up and down the carpet, up and down. His words engaged her less.

"I am sorry," he said. "I do not intend to interfere. But I am so fond of both of you. And I do not understand what it is you *want*. Som is the most easy of persons to understand. He wants you to be *happy*. If it is shopping you want to do, anything like that you wish—"

"Shopping?" she looked up confused.

"Well, whatever you want. More of anything. Trips abroad. The prosperity of Europe, it is fantastic. It is all possible for you now. Every summer you can go. Think of the children's benefits."

Rage had filled her, welled into her eyes and run down her cheeks in tears, looking like weakness.

"Oh, now I have made you cry. Please do not."

Simrit had gone on crying wordlessly, looking out of the window.

Vetter waited diplomatically for her to stop, busying himself with a magazine from the coffee table. When she stopped crying he was still there.

"Don't pay any attention to me," Simrit apologized.

She got up and went to the window. The house was so quiet when the children were at school. The morning spun

81

itself out softly, invisibly. But during this hour between eleven and twelve it held still like gold liquid in a silver cup, the hour of silver and gold. If only she had the peace to match it. Vetter, assured that she was all right now, got up.

"I will go now," he said quietly.

"I'm sorry about my behaviour," said Simrit. "I seem to spend my time apologizing."

"Sometimes," said Vetter, "one cannot cope and then it is best to find out why. Perhaps all you need is a medical checkup. Why not come to Germany when Som makes his next trip?"

"Oh, I don't think so."

"The best medical care will be available."

She shook her head.

"I know. But if everyone rushes to Europe for everything, if the whole universe revolves around Europe, then how's anything to grow in India, in Asia? Who's going to make it?"

"Yes," he conceded, "I have sympathy with that. You have feeling for what is yours and that I understand. Go on, please."

She smiled a little.

"Well that's all really. And I'm not sick."

"Then what is wrong?"

She made a helpless gesture.

"I suppose we cry about things we can't change."

Som and Vetter came home late and exhilarated that evening. There was an intimate, excited camaraderie between the two men, as if they belonged to a secret society. They were in soaring spirits. The children, except the two eldest who were in boarding school, were in bed. It seemed odd to think that fanning out from this immaculate room there were tumbled beds where children slept and the day's doings overflowed from shelves and cupboards onto the floor. But all Som's magnanimity stopped short abruptly here, like a great reservoir dammed and held within this room. Vetter didn't know it never even trickled into any other corner of the house.

The second youngest had been operated the day before to correct her breathing. An intruding hostile particle of bone had been removed from her nose and today the fashionable doctor, blindly cheerful and chattering about his luck at the races, had wrenched the cotton wadding from the small nostril with a suddenness that had stunned the child and sent her spinning and stumbling to her mother. Simrit had been sitting with her until she heard the men arrive, boisterous as boys.

She took a gulp of the vodka Som had put beside her. It burned its way to her stomach and made her cough. This, she heard Som say, was a celebration.

The little girl had not cried. She had borne her ordeal with an extraordinary maturity for her age, a touching stoic dignity. "Are you all right?" Simrit had whispered. And after that first shock the child had given a brief soldier's nod, awakening a kind of awe in Simrit at the life she cared for every day.

"All this stuff," Som motioned to the furniture, "will have to go. We'll get the whole place re-done from top to bottom. The sky's the limit, Simrit, get what you like."

She felt their eyes on her, waiting for her to show her pleasure. But the raised pattern of the blue and russet upholstery, faded in places, felt known and comfortable under her hand. Perhaps she could salvage it for another room where it need not be on display and never be threatened with removal. She smiled her assent.

"What about something for Simrit?" Vetter said with a conspiratorial glance at her. "A piece of jewellery to mark the occasion?"

"You're going to Jaipur," Som said. "Get her a necklace there. She loves the Rajasthani enamel work."

They were soon noisy and gay and she was caught up in their mood and carried along.

Som was telling stories of the funnier aspects of the deal they had been working on. He was laughing so much that half the story was lost. Vetter was roaring, too, not at Som's story which he had heard, but at Som's enjoyment of it. Hilarity soon took over, taking the place of conversation. Simrit joined in.

"What are we celebrating?" she demanded.

The new deal to make armaments. The genius stroke, said Som. They talked about it eagerly in her presence today. It was all wrapped up, an unbelievable combination of luck and perseverence. Over at last were the meetings, the conferences, the long weary hours of lobbying, the phone calls and the entertainment—all that had gone for months into the making of a deal.

"And you walk in here without one flower for your wife," joked Vetter.

Simrit drank more vodka.

"Are you going to advertise?" she asked.

"Advertise what?"

Som came to sit on the arm of her chair. He began stroking her hair and then the length of her bare arm. His touch sent a thrill resembling fear through her.

"I'd like a cigarette," she said.

She didn't want a cigarette. She wanted to be one of them.

"My girl's in the mood to celebrate, too. See Rudy? This

is her once a year or so cigarette. Here, you shall have an imported one."

Som took a slim blue and gold one from a packet marked "Cocktail Colours" that Vetter had brought off the plane and lit it for her. She asked for another vodka. Som was pleased she was joining in.

"But aren't you going to advertise whatever you're making?" she repeated. "Bombs or whatever it is?"

"Not bombs, lady."

Vetter explained it was a weapon to replace the outdated mountain guns in service.

"Well whatever it is," she said nonchalantly. "Aren't you going to? Why don't companies advertise armaments, or do they? Look at everything else that's advertised from underwear to diamond rings, and it's the best ads that get the buyers. Look at me telling you," she began to laugh again. "You're the ones in business."

She couldn't stop laughing. The men exchanged the look of adults over an overwrought child.

"That's an idea, Rudy," Som said and Vetter agreed.

"But how do countries go shopping for arms, Som?" she went on. "Do they look up special journals? There must at least be catalogues with descriptions. How does it all happen? Does't there have to be a guarantee, like for stoves and electric kettles and household appliances? Don't the manufacturers have to say guaranteed lethal, like rat poisons say?"

Som was filling up his glass, Vetter minutely examining the decorative detail in a miniature above the mantlepiece. Simrit pulled herself together and before she drank her second vodka she had a single clear thought: Som and Vetter belong to a world that just goes on perfecting techniques, and I can't bear living in it any more. There must be other worlds.

At the table set with elegant silver Som had brought back from Switzerland or France or somewhere, she presided meticulously. She could see herself doing her unblemished hostessing in the mirror opposite with her queerly static face reflected in it. Her husband poured wine Vetter had brought and she drank it, the courses beginning to blur on her plate. But everything tasted good. Vetter was full of praise for the food and he and Som were eating with appetite. At the corner of her vision a dark shape hovered, not clearly visible in the mirror, neither quite stationery nor quite mobile which, she identified when it came forward as the bearer. Forwards and backwards he moved, like a dark moth with a rhythm but no life of its own. A moth on a string pulled by the food on their plates. She turned in spite of herself to look full at him, to invest him if she could with personality, and at once he was at her elbow, waiting courteously for her command. What have I done for him, she thought aghast, that he should have to do this for me, days without number as long as he can work?

Her image in the mirror was all blurred by that time. The dark moth was hovering and going away to the rhythm of their appetites, the two men were eating and talking, eating and talking. Great highways of culture, she was thinking confusedly, long highroads of achievement—all the knowledge, all the glory slowly eked out of total ignorance—from the accidental striking of flint to a line of lyric poetry or the distance to a star—all of it might be lost as inadvertently as the button off one's coat. Just drop off and disappear. Music and language disappear, and mathematics be reduced to counting notches on a stick—because of men like these, one on either side of her—the envied, successful, appalling creatures of her time, caught up in a sickness they did not even recognize, a spiralling mania for affluence. She was looking at her lemon souffle through tears.

"What is the matter, Simrit?"

Som was up, bending over her.

"She isn't well obviously," he was telling Vetter. "I don't know what has come over her. She's been like this for months."

Vetter was on his feet too, his napkin still under his chin. The dinner party was ended.

"I'm very sorry," she mumbled.

She excused herself and went to her room, lying fully dressed on her bed, telling herself there was no need to tremble and shake. Imagine instead the things that happen in this very city, sometimes just down the road. Imagine the abandoned vagrant children, the days without food, nights without shelter for people with no additional, outer threat over them, no fear of war. Why let imagination travel further than that to some woman with a child in her belly getting Som's and Vetter's bomb, or whatever it was, and flying apart, leaving bits of child and palpitating entrails all over the place. Bits of child that could be exchanged for a whole new drawing room, furniture and upholstery, silk and velvet cushions for gracious and civilized living. Children in their cradles should fear men like you, she said to herself. But that's not what I'm crying about. I've never cried about such things before. It's Som!

The smell of brandy and cigar smoke drifted to her. A long time afterward Som materialized beside her bed. She could feel his presence. In a fantasy the instant before she opened her eyes he stood there holding something in one hand. She sat up and looked at it. It was a common little pink bell-shaped flower. There were lilies like it growing wild in clumps in their garden. As soon as a clump was cleared it would spring up somewhere else. She was terribly glad that Som had brought her this particular flower. She opened her eyes and looked at Som. He had had that vertical frown line ever since she had met him. He had cultivated it then to give himself a maturer look among his older business colleagues. Now it was deep and permanent, poignantly part of their long, long relationship, a thing he could not banish even if he wanted to. She reached out to touch it as he sat down on her bed.

"Feeling better, Sim?" he asked.

"Yes, thank you."

"What happened? What's the matter with you?"

"I'm confused. I'm wretched."

"But what about? You have everything in the world any woman could want." There was a grain of exasperation in his voice.

"Yes I know."

"Then what's the matter? Why do you go on as if you were grief-stricken about something?"

His hair was beginning to grey and thin into strands. She traced his frown line with a light finger, looking at him with a loving, searching desperation. He looked away.

"Well, what is it, Sim?" He glanced at his watch. "Lord, it's midnight already. It didn't matter your breaking down like that tonight with just Rudy there—he knows us so well —but you can't go on weeping all the time."

"No. I'll stop."

"How the devil will you stop?" He shrugged Vetter's shrug. It had become a habit. "You're getting terribly thin. Anyway," he teased, "the children don't want a mother who keeps dissolving into tears for no reason. They'll soon wonder what's happening."

She held on to his hands as if she were drowning.

"Stop crying, Simrit. What on earth is there to cry about? I'm a damned good husband to you, aren't I? What have you got to complain about? We're having a wonderful life and it's going to get better and better."

He got up, hands thrust in his pockets, and talked vehemently, suppressed laughter in his voice.

"Think of it, we can go abroad any time we want, any bloody time, buy anything we want. We can aircondition this whole place, furnish it all over again, and Rudy's right. You ought to have something to mark the occasion. What would you like? You didn't say."

I want a world whose texture is kindly, she thought. Surely there is such a world. After all, people once believed it was flat and it turned out otherwise. If its shape could turn out different, so can its texture.

She began, "Som, the world is so full of violence."

"Yes of course it is. It always has been. Don't tell me that's what you're crying about."

She drew her hand across her eyes.

"I don't mean war—that's far away. I mean people with each other. And look at the arid way we live, without friends."

"What are you talking about? Of course we've got friends. And what's got into you? You've never found anything wrong with the way we've lived all these years."

That's it, she thought. When the whole world is dying it doesn't matter. You don't even notice it till you start dying. And now all she wanted was to get to a clean cold atmosphere where there was some goal beyond self-advancement. Perhaps it had been trying to catch up with her all these years. Well, now it had.

"I don't understand you, but I think you'd better sort it out for yourself or you'll fall ill," said Som.

He disappeared into his dressing room and came back a

few minutes later in his dressing gown.

"Aren't you getting undressed tonight?"

Simrit sat up and swung her legs to the floor.

"Don't now," he said, "it's late."

He lay down beside her, compelling her with his urgency, but it could no longer transport her unresisting to a comfortable place. She stayed separate, excluded, rebellious. Much later she woke unaccountably alone in the night, though Som was asleep in the next bed, his back to her.

A sex life with laws of its own, kept apart from the rest of life, must wake one up on a night such as this with all the doubts and fears of the years knocking against it. Sex was no more just sex than food was just food. Dinner tonight had been so much more, an affair of refinement and ceremony. Even the bowl of roses on the table had been part of dinner. Once the edge was off hunger a meal had to be more than food. And once past its immediacy, sex had its visions too—of tenderness, of humour, of more than a physical act. Sex could be an argument or a problem shared. The same spring fed all its facets—the day's work in office, children at home, bed at night. Simrit felt on the verge of a fatal realization. She was no longer able to follow the goals Som had set for himself, and the inability seemed to be spreading through her veins, affecting the very womb of her desires, drying up the fount within her.

Som was baffled at first and then angered by her behaviour, as if she had attacked his honour.

8

Simrit looked at Som during those days not always recognizing him. He had German phrases on the tip of his tongue and Vetter's mannerisms. He did most of his personal shopping in Europe. In a royal blue jacket, a French silk tie and hand-stitched Roman leather shoes he even looked foreign. That was what he was wearing the night the end came. They were at a restaurant too expensive for the younger crowd, hosting a dinner for eight other couples, their table not too close to the mass of jerking, writhing dancers moving in and out of mauve and copper lighting. Between them their party must have drunk three feet of Scotch before coming here.

Simrit's share had made her calm and remote, letting her listen distantly to talk of Paris, London, Greece, London and Paris.

"Simrit!" Som's frown line was etched deep as he tried to attract her attention from the other end of the table. "I'm trying to order. Are you having tandoori chicken like the rest of us?"

"All right," she said.

We're choked with activity, thought Simrit. Even our belongings never stay still. Magazines made neat blocks on the coffee table at home, pyramids in the godown. They were flipped through undigested, taken away to make room for newer issues, finally sold as junk to the kabariwala at seventy paise per kilo. A huge dreadful cycle of waste. A glut of things accumulated and thrown away with no time to savour any of it. The children were bored and couldn't amuse themselves and Som was thinking of buying TV. We really should look out of the window more often, walk down the road now and then. Cut off from the look, the smell, the feel of things around one, one could become stricken and bereaved.

The tandoori chicken placed before her was lean-fleshed but tender, red peppered, rubbed with lemon juice and fresh ginger. She began to eat it with her fingers. The music coiled swiftly, tightly around them, then expanded slowly, painfully. It coiled and expanded in an unbearable accordion-like tension. It sounded wild and improbable, not a background for gaiety so much as a testimony of impending disaster. She could almost feel it approaching. But disaster or not she must talk. Som at the other end of the table was full of anecdotes, keeping his half of the guests laughing. He was so terribly good socially, only intimacy floored him. Finger bowls of hot water garnished with slices of lemon for greasy fingers were brought. She dipped her fingers into her bowl, squashing the lemon slice between them and wiped them on her napkin.

The big man from Leeds on her right, one of the new people who attended their parties said, " It's amazing what this music can make you do. You don't think you can get up and dance to it, but you do."

Not much education, Som had told her about him, but a genius for multiplying a pound and quite a character. She wished she could remember his name. They turned to watch the dancers perform their ritual, curiously impersonal, each alone. Som, she could see, was signalling her to *talk*. Talk was the missing link between her and Som, between her and his world. She had a famishing need for talk. She was driven to a quiet desperation for want of it. Good talk, about books, events, ideas, people. The Leeds man on her right was still watching the dancers.

"Which d'you think lasts longer between people, sex or friendship?" she asked.

"Oh I say, Som," he bellowed goodnaturedly down the table above the music, "your wife wants to know—"

Laughter swallowed Som's reply. The odd thing was she really wanted to know.

"Well which?" she asked.

He considered it.

"If you ask the youngsters nowadays—my daughter, for instance, she's got her own flat in London—it's all the same thing. They don't keep it in separate compartments any more. They're casual about it, like having a cup of coffee. Why, what's the matter?"

"I was thinking sometimes a cup of coffee is better."

He gave a loud guffaw. "Don't tell your old man that."

"I meant it's a better way to get to know a person."

Why, she went on, was it so hard to get people past the

conventional rut? Once it had been prudery, now it was casual sex—either way it was conventional, just what everyone was doing. When was anybody ever going to start thinking for himself, having a life style of his own?

There, she told herself, I'm talking.

The man from Leeds was staring at her pointedly and she saw that all the others had got up to dance.

"Y'know, Mrs Raman, you're quite a woman."

"Why?"

"I don't know quite. One doesn't expect a person like you to come out with the things you do come out with."

"Like what?"

"Oh c'mon, you know what I mean. An angelic face like that and then you talk all fluent like the Encyclopaedia Britannica. It gave me quite a turn to find out tonight you write books — about rivers and things — and with all those kids you've got. It doesn't match. A little while ago I'm wracking my brains what I should talk to you about and you start up with sex of all things. It doesn't rhyme. Know what I mean?"

Simrit thought a minute.

"No," she said.

The Leeds man laughed heartily.

"I'm really enjoying myself tonight."

"So am I," said Simrit sincerely.

As soon as you really began to talk, it gave you a foothold. The trouble was it didn't last. Everyone they knew came and went. No one stayed—to grow old with them. The singer's voice came clearly over the band in what sounded like a chant, words of limpid purity returning again and again to a melodic refrain. She recognized the song as one the children played at home.

How many ears must one man have

> Before he can hear people cry?
> How many deaths will it take till he knows
> That too many people have died?

Only no one was listening to the words. They were giving their bodies to the beat. Even up against it they didn't hear it.

"Let's dance," said the Leeds man. "No, not these gyrations, my kind of dancing."

They were almost stationery on the dance floor, glued together by the flailing arms and acrobatics around them. Som's new friend's grip was very tight.

"Som's a lucky man," he said.

There were all kinds of luck. Som had certainly had plenty, combined with the brashness it took to get ahead.

"A wife like you, wonderful family — how many have you got?" he bent his head, not catching her answer. "And you look like a girl. How do you do it?"

He was holding her as if consoling himself for some lack.

"The first time I came to your house I thought to myself she's a bloody marvel. All those kids and look at her. You been abroad?"

Simrit shook her head.

"Should go. You'd be a sensation. Mean to say you've never been in London or Paris? What's Som been up to not taking you? Believes in keeping the wife at home, does he?"

She said distinctly, "I haven't wanted to go."

He held her away in astonishment, "You're a bloody marvel."

"But I mean it," She said.

"The shopping's fantastic now in Milan. I took my wife and daughter there last spring and they had the time of their lives."

"Shopping," stated Simrit.

"That's it. Everything under the sun and better than in most places. By the way, I'm bringing a TV out for Som next time I come. Tell me what you'd like me to bring you."

Simrit thought hard against the music.

"I — don't know," she admitted. "Sorry. I'll try and think of something."

The Leeds man guided her back to their table as the music stopped, cupping her elbow.

"You're a bloody marvel, Mrs Raman. Take it from me you are."

It was past midnight again when they got home. Simrit undressed and went to the door of the room to which Som had removed himself a few days earlier. He was wearing a silk dressing gown with a pattern of black and orange diamonds on it and listening from the depths of an armchair to a tape recording of one of his favourite pop singers while he finished his cigar. It was the cigar smoke reaching her room that had given her the courage to come tonight, knowing there would be a relaxed interval before he went to bed.

"Som?"

He didn't turn his head to look at her.

"Yes, what is it?"

"We don't have to live like strangers, do we?"

"Don't start that again."

"Why did you have to move out of our room?"

"You know damned well why."

She sat down on the edge of the sofa-bed. No I don't, she thought. Can't we just hold hands? Can't we lie side by side like brother and sister, like friends, and talk? Can't a husband and wife be friends? Is that forbidden? Can't you be a brother to me, Som, or just a loving stranger until we sort this out? And out of that non-insistence, that non-preying upon each other, something sweet may dawn.

"I wish," she said passionately, "we could be friends."

Som scratched his jaw reflectively.

"Aren't you being a bit melodramatic? Anyway, whatever you're trying to get at, it's quite beyond me."

His tone was detached, his eyes empty, and that, with him, signalled the end. Simrit felt a prickle of terror start at his systematic cutting off. He could do it so thoroughly. She had seen it happen to others, to people they had called their friends. Why had she imagined herself safe? If you're his wife, you're his wife, and if you're not, you're nothing. After that he commits no immorality even if he tramples you under foot because he doesn't know you're there any more.

"I'm not trying to get at anything," she said, her voice unsteady.

"Then you'd better go to bed. It's late and I have to leave for Madras tomorrow."

"I didn't know — "

"I'll be away about a week. That should give you enough time to think things over. You're supposed to be good at that. And you'd better decide what you want to do, get on with a normal life or finish this farce once and for all."

The ultimatum stunned her. She knew intuitively that he had gone much further in his own mind than thinking things over. He had settled the matter. She heard herself going on incoherently about it, unable to stop.

He cut her short, "Look, I don't understand that high-flown stuff. And God knows you've had enough time. I want an answer when I get back. A plain one I can understand."

He switched off the tape. He got up, stretched and yawned, already complete without her, on his way to a new chapter. He turned off the top light and only the strong desk lamp remained, throwing the rest of the room into shadow.

In the sudden darkness her mind leapt to solutions, miraculous ones that jump barriers at the sound of a voice, the turn of a phrase.

"Som."

"What?"

"Som, do you have to go away tomorrow?"

"Yes."

"I can't believe this is happening."

"You know damned well why it's happening. When a woman freezes up every time her husband touches her it's time to call it a day."

She cried out, "It isn't true. I miss you!"

She stood in the unresponsive dark feeling as if she had been pitched into an indifferent outer nothingness cut off from light and sound. Then she turned into the corridor, groping her way to her room, staying close to the wall like the newly blind. The next day she had gone to see Raj.

9

Tree shade fell like patterned lace on the road the day she went to see Raj. Fresh red paint on the letter box at the corner gave it a wet bright glow. It was the sort of mellow day that made colours look more brilliant. Delhi had a drowsy spring warmth before the heat struck it like a vicious blow. Simrit was not sure where Raj lived. She had never been to his house, though she had met him at crowded impersonal parties after their first meeting at the discussion group. Even in a crowd he managed to create magnetic little islands of interest around him. He was known in and outside Parliament for an unrelenting concern with everything he trained his mind on. And he could talk. Before she noticed the way he stood or smiled or his typical gesturing, she was attracted by his talk. There was such a wealth of it, of ideas she could see taking shape before her eyes. Not a re-hash of other people's views but rough-hewn stars of his own invention, carelessly offered to the company around him to polish if they cared to. He wore his ideas with the same slight arrogance that other men wore perfect clothes. Once she had actually made her way across the room to hear what he was saying to the people near him. He seemed to collect people. Without knowing it he had "collected" her. She wasn't a person who crossed a room or made a special effort to talk to anybody. There had been something symbolic in her room crossing, in stepping out and proclaiming she was there. But this was different. She had nothing to give today. She felt nerve-wracked and inwardly bruised, but sure she had not mistaken the affinity between them.

Raj had one unit of a compact semi-detached house on Pandara Road with a pocket handkerchief lawn of smooth uninterrupted green, except for a single tree in regal scarlet blossom. He sat in a reclining chair on the grass, reading. There was a blue pottery bowl on the grass beside him containing cigarette butts. A mess of newspapers around his chair reminded her it was Sunday. He got up when he saw her and swung another chair out from the verandah. He was obviously used to starting without preamble and she wondered whether he would pick up his book again and go on reading.

"I've interrupted your afternoon," she said. "I'm sorry."

"You needn't be," he put a marker in his book and placed it on the grass beside him. "Do you want a cup of tea?"

The direct quality she had noticed at parties was even more pronounced and disturbing here. She could not melt away from it into a crowd or take refuge in politenesses. She felt alive and tense, too many antennae quivering. She refused his offer of tea, suddenly awkward as a schoolgirl.

"Do you smoke?" he held out his pack.

"No."

Raj lit one unhurriedly for himself and smoked half of it in silence.

"What do you do when you're agitated or under a strain?"

She frowned. "I don't know. Why should one do anything in particular? I suppose I do some work, write."

He was leaning back in his chair, his fingers interlocked behind his head, looking at her appraisingly.

"Yes, I suppose you would."

She was annoyed, defensive. "Why should that be odd?"

"Well, the whole point when you're under a strain is to get away from your usual routine, break out. You bury yourself in some more routine. I wonder," he went on, "what you're avid about?"

"Avid? Why must one be avid about anything? I'm avid, if you insist, about restraint."

She was on the verge of quarreling. Raj on the other hand looked relaxed and amused.

"Yes I'm sure you are," he grinned. "I wonder how that works out in general living."

"Very well," she said coolly. 'It has for thousands of years."

"Has it? Somehow I don't think it has brought this country many dividends, this Hindu avidity for restraint. It's compromise with everything outside the sanctum and sheer rigidity within."

"If it hadn't compromised where do you think Hindu culture would be today?"

"That's true. But you don't need to be like that any more.

There's no battle for cultural survival on now. This is your own country and your own culture is in charge. It's time to break out and be avid, be *something*."

"That's a matter of opinion," she said ruffled.

Raj continued to study her affably through a cloud of smoke.

"I have to go," she said, getting up.

Raj was up before her, his hands on her shoulders restraining her.

"Sit down, Simrit. You've just come."

His casual use of her name, as if he had known her a long time, had a calming effect on her. She sank back, resting her head against the wooden frame of her chair.

"It's a problem you or someone should write about," he said when he was comfortably settled again. "What is absent from this Hindu civilization of yours is avidity, the positive desire for something positive. You have to unearth that, and if your principles don't help you to, find some that do. Restraint is a fine thing but at this particular juncture in our history when we have to act, and be responsible for our actions, I think passion and deeds would serve us better."

Simrit said nothing.

"I grant you every civilization has its own key to happiness," he went on. "But if it isn't eating and drinking and the pleasures of the flesh, at least be joyful about abstinence."

Simrit pulled up a handful of grass with difficulty, getting dirt under her nails, and started to sort and arrange the blades according to their size in her lap. The stillness had many sounds, a taxi grinding its gears as it turned a corner, distant shouts from the public playground, a single noted monotonous birdcall announcing the approach of summer. She did not know why she had come; but she knew her being here was not another unrelated segment of the afternoon.

When she glanced up he was still unhurriedly looking.

"End of lecture," he smiled.

"Why do you talk about this country as if you were a foreigner?" she asked.

"That happens when you belong to a minority. You look at things from the outside. You don't take them for granted, you keep sounding them out. You get more anxious about them. They have to measure up all the time. Maybe because if they don't, people like oneself—the different ones—get thrown on the dungheap."

"I can't see what difference it would make being in a minority."

No she wouldn't, thought Raj, secure as she is in her ancestors. Her assurance came from knowing in her bones where she belonged. Those like her, the huge Hindu majority, drew their credentials from an old deep source. Confronted with a problem, the whole person, not a divided being like his, faced it and gave it not just the light of one mind but of a culture. That was the trouble, too. When the culture was like hers, unchanging, lots of problems remained unfaced. It made Raj wonder whether a Hindu ever tackled a problem as an individual. Did Hindus have any feelings that were personal and private, unconnected with institutions like the family, caste, and the beaten track of these past 2,000 years and more?

Simrit would not know about his breed of people, products of a revolt, who began with themselves, without the cushion of a past. Like the rich with their riches the Hindu took his credentials for granted. It was an astonishing brand of vested interest, this unshakeable assumption of superiority before which new ideas reared away like wild creatures from the threat of harness. Education and persuasion made no dent in this picture. Raj, not part of any cosy set-up, had no alternative but to survey it from the outside. Simrit, he noticed, had got up to go and look at his tree.

Raj had no family either. His parents had died in an accident soon after he left university, and the house he had been born in was now in Pakistan. He never stopped marvelling at his father. Thrown out of his home at nineteen for his conversion to Christianity, the boy had gone penniless and nameless—he had had to change that too—into the world, braving the rough emotional weather of an immigrant on his own soil, to become one of the oustanding men in his community. Most of his reserves had been used up in the formidable fight against tradition. But Raj, even as a child, had not been able to identify himself completely with his father's revolt. He had been too conscious of the older heritage around them, the Hindu mainstream of the country's life. It intrigued and fascinated him, this environment to which his blood belonged, though much in it clashed ruggedly with his upbringing. Besides, being a Christian before independence had sounded disloyal. It had meant being tied to the religion and culture of the West when freedom had been the country's cry. Oddly, the withdrawal of the British had changed all that and Christianity had become Indian, its schools and colleges and hospitals firmly part of the community.

He remembered his father best at family prayers, when he prayed aloud, pouring out his whole being through each detail of his day to the God he worshipped, in a voice whose every inflection proclaimed the faith behind it. There was something awe-inspiring about a man so sure of the love of God. Raj had been a little afraid of him. But he had loved his mother and because of her had become an ardent lover of life and a strong and immediate reactor to human beings. Books, as a result, had never moved him, except at times poetry. Nor did ordinary social contact and entertainment

People did and lastingly. "Earth's the right place for love. I don't know where it's likely to go better." The line he had once quoted to Shaila went through his head.

He and Shaila had been devouringly in love four years earlier, until their plans had been wiped clean out by a single forseen turn of events, one they had often discussed: her parents' choice of a husband for her. The time they had spent together, always in hiding, for she had insisted on secrecy, had a dreamlike quality now. It had been like possessing a woman who kept her face covered, tantalizing, never quite satisfying. Under the mantle of secrecy she imposed he had never fully known her. Ever since, he had discarded violent emotion as untrustworthy. There had to be more. He knew he himself was capable of much more. All his worthwhile associations had a terrifying longevity. But their physical passion for each other had not allowed anything else to grow. And in that state she had not been able when the crisis came, to face her family with the announcement that she wanted to marry a Christian. A violent, irrational passion could be violently, irrationally disowned.

A change of mind or heart he could have understood, but not the death-dealing incapacity that had paralyzed her at the moment of decision. She had disowned him utterly. And not satisfied with that she had gone on retracting little by little all she had felt for him until one day not long after it was over she actually believed she had never loved him. The whole thing had never happened. It had been an illusion. But then so was the whole tumultous, actual world according to the Hindu. Even your hand was not your hand, your pain was not your pain in that indisputable, flawless, monstrous logic.

His equilibrium had returned with painful slowness. His own feeling for her had been deeper-based, fully analysed.

Given time it would have matured, but in their rapacity perhaps what they had had was plunder, not love. The debacle with Shaila had helped him decide he would stand for Parliament. He was certain that any Indian who had the capacity to think and act must use it in a big constructive way or a whole civilization would crumble under mould.

Simrit came back.

"Sit down," he invited, "or are you in a hurry?"

"It's so peaceful here. I'd like to stay for hours. I'm tired of eating and drinking and entertaining. I've been doing a lot of that lately."

He looked at the evenness of her colour wherever her skin showed, from her forehead to her feet in their white sandals, down her arms to the tips of her fingers. He saw a woman beautifully clothed and kept, guardian of a full-blown life, lived, scarred and experienced. The preference of many men he knew for the virginal and untouched seemed empty and superficial by comparison. He did not wonder at Simrit's presence in his garden. Most unusual encounters were a gift from the gods. And he liked the complete lack of artifice that had brought her here. It was obvious she was looking for something her own circle could not provide.

Simrit sat down and to her surprise began to talk about her daughter. She was worried, she said, about the packet of letters she had found from a boy she had never approved and Som disliked.

"But it doesn't seem right to forbid a girl of fifteen," she said.

It was part of the unexpectedness of the afternoon that she was talking to this man, a bachelor, about her growing daughter, asking him, of all people how to cope.

"It's quite a problem," Raj agreed.

Som, if knew of it, would be furious, Simrit told him.

Then Som did not know. A Christian home would be different, Raj told himself. The moral lapse of a daughter would be no worse than a son's.

"Unless the boy is really a bad lot, why not let her write to him as long as the correspondence isn't secret and can be shared with you?"

Simrit was relieved at the suggestion. "Yes I'll do that. Love at fifteen is so hard to cope with."

"Is it easier at another age?"

"I don't know," she said shocking herself.

But how few people did know. They pretended to because they couldn't bear to admit it hadn't come their way, neither the pain nor the pleasure of it. The human race was stunted for lack of it, for want of a feeling not eroded by time or change. If that was love, she hadn't found it. A tender understanding of her daughter stirred her.

"Were you in love at fifteen?" Raj asked.

"Yes, but not in the way youngsters now would understand. It was a very romantic attachment. We held hands and kissed a bit—not much and rather chastely, and yearned a lot. I remember my parents were terribly upset and wanted to know "how far" it had gone. I didn't even know what they meant. And now that sort of thing seems to have gone out of life. And a purely sex attraction is such a barrier to getting to know anyone. I was trying to explain that to a man from Leeds last night."

"A man from Leeds?

"Yes, and he didn't get my point."

"What did he say?"

"He kept saying I was a bloody marvel," said Simrit.

Their shared enjoyment brought her perilously close to tears. Not now, she warned herself, struggling for control.

Raj said quietly, "Is there anything I can do?"

She shook her head quickly, recovering herself, and got up. They stood looking at each other, Simrit bewildered that this recognition, like a shaft of broad daylight in a gloomy interior, could arrive in the middle of the other battle she was fighting. She would have to learn what it meant, if there was enough of her left to learn with—afterward. But when she next saw Raj she was dimmed and shaken as though she had been in a wreckage.

10

The room rocked gently back and forth, gradually swaying
to a stop. Blue and gold curtains, blue and gold coverlets
neatly folded on the carved teak chest against one wall, floated
into focus. He could have been in any half-dark, drowsily
warm, sumptuously furnished interior in time or space. He
was, however, in Room 930 of the Intercontinental Hotel in
what, for want of a better name, was known as the Blue and
Gold Suite. It was the corner suite kept for special friends
of the management, no questions asked. And it was morning.
The morning furthermore of November the fifteenth, of the
conference in the Ministry to choose between the three oil

exploration offers that had been with the Ministry for five months. With the discovery of oil in the Jammu region, the decision could no longer be delayed. What had possessed him to stay here all night?

Sumer Singh sat up. The movement jarred the bones of his skull, each one of which felt separately, painfully tender. He eased his legs out of bed very carefully. He did not want to jerk his head again. His head and body felt unconnected, his body well-slept and relaxed, his head throbbing like an engine gone wrong. His feet explored the luxurious pile of lavishly patterned Amritsar carpet. Where in hell were his shoes and socks? He would have to look down. The effort of lowering his head to look for them felt like having an oil drill driven through it, reminding him again of the meeting he was to chair in two hours' time. The search for his shoes gave him a roaring headache. The bold flowered forest and animals woven into the carpet, colourful even in this indeterminate light, collided reminiscently with his gaze. He and Pixie had played some kind of game on it that he for the life of him could not remember. Not cards. Some other damned game. And why in hell on the carpet?

There must have been something hideously wrong with the whisky he had drunk to make him pass clean out like that, because he hadn't drunk all that much. There had been the two of them and as Pixie was a small drinker the bottle of Dimple Scotch still stood half full on the dressing table. There it was, label and all, unmistakeable in its shape, bought at a dealer's in Connaught Place for a hundred and forty blasted rupees, only obviously it hadn't been Scotch. Some mucky inferior stuff. Prohibition in Bombay had started some artistic bootlegging techniques all over the country, including the injection of local brew into bottles of Scotch. Nowadays you never knew for sure what you were getting

The phrase came to his mind as one not his own. Nowadays were the only days he knew. What his father nostalgically referred to as "the old days"—the golden days of zamindari, of plentiful servants, and of cheap plentiful Scotch, also of law and order in the land—the days when gentlemen had money and bounders didn't—had been Sumer Singh's nursery days. Sumer Singh was young by Ministerial standards, forty this year and picked out for a junior Ministership after the last election.

His father, poor man, still trying to distinguish gentleman from bounders, would never, not if it had been the last hotel in Delhi, have stayed at the Intercontinental. It did not matter that it was the most elegant, beautiful and best run hotel in town, the one that measured most glitteringly up to international standards. According to his father only black money and expense accounts booked there, not counting foreigners of course. An Indian gentleman took himself to more sedate surroundings. On his infrequent visits to the capital he stayed at the shabby genteel Imperial, where he would sit in the side garden in view of the towering dusty palms that lined the entry to the hotel, drinking Flowery Orange Pekoe and gossiping with people fit to associate with. The current crop of politicians did not rank among them. He would be there now and sometime today he would expect Sumer Singh to call on him.

Sumer Singh wondered what time Pixie had left. There was no trace of her, he noted approvingly, not a speck of powder, not a stray hair in the wash basin, not even the damp imprint of a hand on one of the snowy white towels on the towel rail. She seemed to appear and disappear at the clap of his hands, an ideal arrangement. He wasn't even sure where she lived, though he had made it possible for her to get the flat ahead of several dozen others on a waiting list.

He dressed and went out into the corridor. Luckily there was no one about and he went down unseen to the taxi stand at the side entrance. There was no bill to settle. The suite was kept for his exclusive use and he generally used it twice a week by appointment with Pixie. The Sikh driver, reaching back from his seat to swing open the door of the taxi for him enquired, "One hundred Willingdon Crescent?" Sumer Singh hid the unpleasant jolt this gave him. No Minister could be anonymous for long in Delhi and he had been using this side entrance for three months, though he had always kept his own car before and left long before morning. The taxi driver's cool impersonal eyes watched him off and on in the mirror. Scrutiny did not worry Sumer Singh. A man who had campaigned with flair and won an election did not worry if someone looked his way. Besides he was unusually good looking. Thick wavy hair, expressive hazel eyes and chiselled features adorned a face whose chief charm was its boyish candour. It was a face even smudgy newsprint could not spoil. But the taxi driver's look was not the kind he was used to, and close proximity with what Sumer Singh identified as one of "a crowd" was something even electioneering had not accustomed him to.

The election had been his first achievement. He had attended a well-known public school in the days before competitive exams had cut away all but the high mark earners, and gone to college before education for the masses had tossed pedigree to the four winds. He had done poorly in both institutions and had later failed the entrance exam to the Foreign Service which his father had insisted on his taking now that zamindari had been abolished. He had been thinking of going into the films himself when the offer of a Congress ticket had come his way. The ruling Party's attention had been flattering and politics had opened up possibilities that films would not have done. He would not on his own have dreamed of entering politics, but here it was accidentally his career. And in the months since his Ministership particularly, he had developed an astonishing degree of aplomb. The mastery of facts and figures had however never been in his line. Sumer Singh had always avoided homework and the Petroleum Ministry had a plethora of it.

He started to get restive as the taxi cruised along the empty early morning road at a calculatedly leisurely pace. He wanted to tell the driver to speed up, but he found the man's cool indifference unnerving. If a man knew where you were going, and therefore who you were, he would normally have a friendly remark or two to make, just the time of day if no other. He would not sit there steering blank-faced, and Sumer-Singh suspected, with deliberate maddening slowness. His father would have known how to deal with him. His father had never suffered from class confusion, tolerated no nonsense from servants, and they had served him devotedly. Including the doddering old valet, now on his last legs, who never left his employer's side. But then his father had never tolerated what he called nonsense from anyone, not even his son. Sumer Singh was certain that if there was one person in India totally unimpressed by his Ministership and the political future it had opened up before him, it was his father. He was uncomfortably compelled to add the driver as a second. He felt ill-at-ease in the presence of both, as if what he had done showed. He was irritated and unprepared for the morning meeting ahead of him. He told himself he would be more careful in future. His overnight stay was a lapse he had never permitted himself before and it had happened only because his wife and children were away for the children's holidays visiting her parents. Anyway, in his stale head-heavy condition Pixie did not interest him and it was time he terminated the arrangement.

He had to hurry when he got home. Bahadur, his personal servant, efficient as usual, was waiting with morning tea and hot water for his shave and bath, and fresh clothes had been laid out. There was a message too, to say that the Senior Minister wanted Sumer Singh to call on him at the Willingdon Nursing Home at eight. He had expected the summons. The day was getting crammed full before it had begun. Sumer Singh knew he had to talk to Bahadur one of these days about the hanky-panky going on in the servants' quarters. His security men had told him his personal servant was involved in a racket selling crates of Scotch he bought cheaply through his contacts at an embassy, and was making money on the side in other worse ways. It did not help the Minister of a prohibition-plank Government to have this kind of talk getting about, apart from whatever else he was up to. He'd have to warn the man on pain of dismissal to stop that activity.

When he re-entered his dressing room his discarded clothes had been taken away. His wallet of soft brown leather initialled in gold lay on the dressing table and beside it two round pink plastic counters and a yellow one of the sort used in children's games. He picked them up mystified and then remembered the game he and Pixie had played. Tiddly winks of all idiotic things. Absent-mindedly he put them in his pocket, on edge now to leave and have the interview with his Minister done with. He could hear the driver revving up the engine before he drove the car round to the front to take him to the Willingdon Nursing Home. Bahadur, looking smart as a pin, stood in the doorway. Too bloody smart with that bootlegging racket going on.

"Yes what is it?" said Sumer Singh irritably.

"Is there anything else you require, sir?"

Sumer Singh was feeling better after tea and a hot bath, but he was in no mood to deal with corruption in the servants' quarters. Anyway, the fellow was a competent servant and there was no point in rushing into reprimand. He'd mention it some other time.

"No. And I will have breakfast on my return."

The Willingdon Nursing Home never looked clean. The entrance was not properly swept and there was no crisp, starched antiseptic atmosphere. Sumer Singh strode through the anteroom past a motley collection of people waiting at the out-patients' section. He carefully guarded his disgust. He went along the verandah that ran the length of the private rooms to the end room where the Minister for Petroleum lay. There was no nurse about but it was eight o'clock, the time he had been given, and he walked in. The Minister lay propped up on pillows looking haggard and ill. The skin of his hands, clasped slackly on the sheet, was too loose for his knuckles. His eyes were closed. Sumer Singh sat down on a straight-backed chair near the bed wishing he had had some breakfast. The man opened his eyes. They looked colourless. Eyes seemed to fade, like skin and hair, with age.

The old man—popularly known as Sardar Sahib—leader—for the massive common sense he had long embodied—saw Sumer Singh half rise in greeting and closed his eyes again. These days the images behind his closed eyes seemed nearer than what he saw when he opened them. And the images were all of the past, of the dawn of independence twenty years earlier, a new age without the experience in modern technology to master it. Freedom—and the mighty reality of hundreds of millions unversed in it. He had not been to Harrow and Cambridge like the Prime Minister. He had been schooled mostly in hardship and till he was nearly adult and earning he had seldom known the satisfaction of a square meal. He had little enough in common with the Prime Minister in taste and temperament, too. But there was between them the indestructible bond of men who have shared adventure and who feel invincible in the face of odds. And if one quality was needed to face this kind of freedom it was invincibility. And planning. They had drawn up a plan to utilize resources when they were much younger men, long before India's future had been placed in their hands. Now the time had come to put it into action.

"How would you like the oil portfolio?" the Prime Minister had asked him.

"What oil? "he had retorted. "There is no Indian owned oil"

Oil production entire was less than half a million tons, and the three companies, British and American, who produced it, fed the Indian market with products they brought from West Asia at the price that suited them. Refinery agreements with them had been signed that year of 1951 on hard terms, for India had not been in a position to bargain. They had said it would be ruinously expensive for India to start full-scale exploration for oil. Nor had it seemed suitable to leave oil exploration entirely to them. So what oil was the Prime Minister talking about?

The Prime Minister had turned to the map covering the wall behind him. It had marked on it the natural resources of India, the scarcely tapped wealth of a subcontinent waiting for Indian initiative. The natural growth of a nation, interrupted by two hundred years of foreign occupation, had to be resumed now, he was saying. He pointed to a potential oilbearing area of about four hundred thousand square miles for which exploration would have to be mapped out and help obtained.

"If the oil companies will not help us," said the Prime

Minister, "we'll have to find someone who will. That is where the oil portfolio comes in."

Sardar Sahib had brightened at the prospect of a battle. "I'll take it," he had said.

The Prime Minister had looked at him, amusement in his eyes, a brother-to-brother look Sardar Sahib knew well.

"I thought you would. I might tell you though that I haven't even been able to interest the Planning Commission in the search for oil. It's not going to be easy for you."

Sardar Sahib thought briefly: Isn't it like him to give me the dirty work, the grind, just because he knows I'll do it. Because he knows I am tough and tenacious and I'll never give up.

No one knew it better than the Prime Minister. There was going to be a blast of opposition as the main emphasis of development swung away from agriculture to heavy industry, and Sardar Sahib, the toughest of the freedom fighters was the one to weather it. This was a peasant country, people would say, and agriculture logically should have pride of place. Besides the country needed grain. But the Prime Minister knew it needed something else even more, the vision of a life different from the one it had known, the vision of a future that only science could produce. People would always grow food—of necessity—and what was not grown could be imported, but no people could face the future in a science-dominated world without science and not put their freedom in jeopardy again. Men needed food, it was true, but they fought for their dreams, dreams that had to be planted now in this dawn of freedom if they were to take root, grow and become part of the Indian air. They—the band that had taken India to freedom—had to see to this before they died. They had to leave the basic structure of industry behind them—the new temples, the Prime Minister called them—

and there were not many years left. To be free but growing old was a terrible challenge.

Sardar Sahib took the portfolio. He set up an oil department,
formulated an oil policy and started the search for oil. He
had to fight, as the Prime Minister had warned, the Planning
Commission as well. The First Plan had not allotted a penny
to oil exploration in spite of the Prime Minister's own enthusiasm for the subject. But finally things had got going. And the
help when it came had come from the Communist world.
Sardar Sahib had bought a Rumanian drilling rig displayed at
an Industrial Fair in Delhi. And he had contracted with
Rumania for personnel to operate it. That was the beginning
of India's oil era. Later they had got equipment and training
facilities from the Soviet Union to start oil exploration.

Another clear image of those years crossed Sardar Sahib's
mind, of himself standing on an exploration site wrapped in an
excitement as intense as any he had ever known. The derrick
looked so alien, so determinedly man-made in that barren
vastness, two hundred feet of iron rising skeletally against
the huge expanse of brilliant blue sky. He was looking at one
for the first time, thinking that *that* was the thing he had
to acquaint himself with. That, and the other paraphernalia
of drilling. Not that he was required to visit sites, but the
job had him under its spell. A feeling close to physical appetite had flooded him as he thought of himself and the men
on the site out there to extract what this 20,000 square feet of
ground had to offer. If it was there, as they believed it was.
If. . . .

For that redoubtable "If" risks had to be taken and while
he took them, the press and the planners were after him like
a pack of hounds baying for his blood. Year after year there
had not been nearly enough results to justify effort and expense. Oil, steel, hydroelectric power were mammoth enter-

prises needing mammoth resources and know-how from wherever it could be bought on the most acceptable terms possible. He would have gone to the devil incarnate if the devil had sold him an oil rig on self-respecting terms. He never got tired of saying there was no room for ideology in a country's development. They had to get the know-how fast from wherever they could. There was hostility to the big projects and it had to be fought in Parliament and in public. People wanted results today. Hardly anybody had had the vision to work for tomorrow, work sometimes in the dark for the gamble that might pay. But blessedly he had had a free hand to do his work.

He had led a delegation to Britain and America and come back empty-handed. But it had been useful. He had felt the breath of the giants and he had returned in a fury of obstinacy and determination. It had been important before but from then on his mission had taken on a sense of destiny. He had faced the world's most powerful combine, the Super State—the oil cartel—and he had broken its monopoly in India. After that he had begged and borrowed, waxed eloquent, arrogant and humble by turns, stormed, raged and pleaded and worked like a demon to obtain the men, the equipment and the know-how that India had to have to build her own refineries and supply her own needs. The climax had come in September 1958 when oil was struck in Cambay. No foreign expert had assessed the site very highly but the Indian geologists in the team had kept hammering at it in their reports. It had turned out to be a big gas find, not an oil field. But a turning point all the same, because Sardar had been certain that if the first few holes drilled had proved dry, the search for oil in the public sector would have been given up. Cambay had been crucial because it had led them to other oilfields in the region: Ankleshwar, which turned out to be a good oil find, and Kalol and other areas.

Sardar Sahib stirred and sighed. To catch up with a world a century ahead in technology had been the fever of his generation, catch up, get going and have something solid to pass on to younger hands and brains. He had held the oil portfolio for eleven years through two general elections, and then resigned for reasons of failing health. And last year he had been persuaded to take it again. He had not wanted to. He knew that there were political changes coming and he was a stop-gap. It would not have been good enough earlier but ill health had queerly sharpened his faculties, revived his fierce loyalty to a man now dead and the goal they had both worked for. So he accepted.

The goal still mattered. He had discovered lying in bed these weeks that when everything else receded and shrank in importance, even the fact of how long one had to live, the goal was there as it had been all his life, steadfast and constant, changing only in its outward aspect: first the star of freedom and then the great grinding challenge of development. The goal was nothing less than the continuation of Indian history, the soul's continued longing to see India fulfil herself, and in the hands of the new Government it seemed to him endangered. He had said so in his crisp blunt fashion and he had quickly noticed a change toward himself. The new Prime Minister had not publicly broken with him but he had noticeably cooled. And then grave illness had struck, putting Sardar Sahib out of action and giving Sumer Singh full charge.

Sardar Sahib opened his eyes and looked at the neat, youthful figure on the chair, not recognizing him immediately. He called himself back from the past. The future was here in this man, his deputy, in whom he had no confidence.

"Shall I come back after the meeting, sir?" asked the younger man.

The Minister's attention riveted on him.

"Certainly not," he said sharply. "I am awake. I particularly wanted to see you before the meeting."

Sumer Singh's headache was on the mend. He arranged his features to look respectful.

"The doctors have not permitted me to study the offers in detail. You have, of course, done that."

That act of speaking seemed to revive the Minister and gave his colourless eyes a metallic brilliance it was not easy to avoid.

"Yes sir," Sumer Singh acknowledged.

The Minister felt extremely doubtful that this was the case.

He said, "It is important to understand that we are in a very different position in oil today than we were twenty years ago and you've got to keep this difference in mind. Our future policy must depend on this fact."

What did oil policy have to do with the offers in hand? The old fossil might have time to waste. Sumer Singh did not. He knew this was a superfluous interview but it was one of the irritating details that had to be attended to for the sake of what was to follow. He had been instructed there was to be no direct clash with the Minister. He hated the whole tone of the proceedings, feeling like a schoolboy under the stern eye of a master who stood no nonsense. Reaching for his handkerchief he found the tiddlywinks counters in his pocket. They seemed to be following him around. He stowed them down deep as far as they would go and looked at the Minister with concentration. It was what he did when he was thinking hard about something else. It had just struck him that in last night's muddle he had invited Pixie to lunch at his house. And he must prevent that at all costs. He wondered what else he had promised her and why in hell he had got so involved with her. She was by no means the most exciting of his pleasurable sexual encounters, but desire quickened now as he thought of her. Pixie dressed was ordinarily pretty with a kind of winsome appeal about her. It was Pixie undressed who had captivated him with her unexpected seventeen-year-old breasts, small, round and exquisite—Pixie who was twenty-five years old and widowed, with a five-year-old child he had never seen. The two faces of woman, he thought, recalling her breasts, the one on view and then this other, concealed, never quite what you expected. There were women whose breasts were just part of their bodies and others—but he had known no others except Pixie's whose were a perpetual wonder, looking like something very young and untouched in the world's springtime. He decided he would not wind up the affair with Pixie just yet. Things were going swimmingly. And what was all the hurry?

Besides, he mused, it was not just her body. She was cheerful and optimistic, and he loathed gloomy people around him. She never made a nuisance of herself, never asked a favour. She was always asking him about himself and his work, how he had enjoyed a press luncheon, what he had said to a student meeting. But what finally counted was her awe of him, some magic she seemed to attach to the fact that he was a "leader". To her that meant a man of dedication. He had never roused this reaction in any personal relationship and it grew on him like a drug. Her curiosity about him was eager and genuine. She made him feel that of all the impossible wonders life might hold, meeting him had been the greatest. Through him—had she been able to put it that way—she was connected with the living heartbeat of the nation, with millions and millions of people stretching away to far coastlines and mountains. For a nice little nobody Pixie had quite an imagination. He realized the Minister was waiting for him to say something. He tried to recall what the old man had been saying. Something about the difference between now and twenty years ago.

Sumer Singh said mechanically, "Now we produce over forty per cent of our crude needs and nearly all our product needs—bitumen and motor spirits, high-speed diesel oil and so on. Where we are still deficient is in the highly sophisticated lubricating oils."

"Yes," said the Minister after a long pause. "Well we still face two difficulties: know-how and quantity. We do not know at this stage if we shall ever produce enough for all our needs. Our plants for the lubricating oils aren't yet in production. It will depend on our oil reserves and those are still—even with the new discovery—a question mark. The second point concerns the competing demands on our foreign exchange. How much can we afford? And the third point is to what extent we can make use of the foreign companies already established here. We have got to a position now in oil where we are no longer grossly dependent, and we must use the future business prospects of these foreign companies as a lever for getting the technology and the investment we lack. The Indian market is expanding. There is plenty of business for them to share. We have to let them share it and to make a proper straightforward business deal with them. The past, you must understand, is over. We are dealing with today's needs."

Pixie had no telephone. He would have to wait till she got to work. By that time he would be in his meeting and afterwards it might be too late. But there was no way round it, he would have to leave it till afterwards. The thought of Pixie arriving at his house panicked him. He decided to leave a message at home that callers should be told he would not be back for lunch.

The Minister was saying, "We must allow the British and American companies expansion in the traditional products, petrol, diesel etc. provided they give us a programme of investment in new products and the assurance of know-how."

Sumer Singh's instructions were to listen and come away, not to inject any argument of his own. No crack in the structure till the time came. But he could not help commenting.

"But that means accepting foreign investment here—more than policy permits—and profits going out of the country."

"Exactly," said the Minister dryly, "and as you rightly surmise there will be a noise against it. We will simply have to face the music."

Sumer Singh nodded. His own interpretation was quite different. Popularity in politics depended on backing, on the cheer from the crowd—any crowd but in large number—and if he was shortly going to become a target for attack, an anti-people man letting profits leave the country, it was going to cut the ground from under him. He had no intention of risking his political life. Nor would there be any necessity to.

The Minister spoke sharply, "If it is rapid development we want there is no time to cater to whims and slogans. Our emphasis so far has been to exclude foreign companies, because they would not help us when we first needed them. Now we will have to allow them expansion, at least recognize the principle of it for our own good."

"The exploration offers before us," reminded Sumer Singh delicately.

He had been here half an hour already listening to a lecture on policy.

"Yes," said the Minister, "we have got to get *neutral* help for the Jammu region."

"Neutral?" repeated Sumer Singh.

"Neither Russian nor American. Jammu is too near our border. It is a security risk. Both these countries have heavily armed Pakistan and are continuing to. The Canadian offer is the best general one. The details you will have to work out."

"We have already contracted with the Soviet Union for off-shore exploration on the west coast," Sumer Singh pointed out.

"The west coast is a long way from the border," said Sardar Sahib acidly. He continued, "The point to be certain of is that we do not surrender any oil in the contract. People who explore normally want a share in oil. That on no account can be allowed."

Sumer Singh said nothing.

Sardar Sahib felt the unaccustomed sensation of fear. Something was amiss. He had been too long in government and in power himself not to sense the tenor of Sumer Singh's entire reaction since he had entered this room. If I could walk, he thought in sudden anguish, if I could only will myself to get up and walk, and be there myself. But he could not even sit up without help, much less walk. A man could only do the best in one's time, and his time was up. He had to come to terms with the fact. But something in him wept at the thought of giving the verdict of the coming meeting into the hands of the man beside his bed. He had believed Sumer Singh incompetent but he had never mistrusted him till today. Sumer Singh, he reminded himself, was the future. But how had such a future arisen out of such a past?

The Minister told Sumer Singh he could go and felt an immediate relief. He had, he believed, a tireless capacity for work, but it had always exhausted him to deal with men of shallow grasp. The interview had begun and ended with a parade of his own viewpoint. All along he had known that the words he was saying were not for his listener. The productive partnership was a process in which two or more people merged. He had experienced it with the men on the sites, with the engineers and even the labourers. He had never felt it for a moment with Sumer Singh. A man of Sumer Singh's calibre in Government was an indication of how Sardar Sahib and his generation had failed. They had built up no trained dedicated cadre in the party to take over. Sumer Singh was not a leader and never would be. He was an election gambit that had worked.

Sardar Sahib's eyes travelled over the uneven whitewash of the walls and through the window he could see that the yard needed cleaning. The nurse when she came in would look as if she needed a scrubbing. God knew if she had sterilized the thermometer she would put into his mouth or properly washed and dried the glass in which she would bring him fruit juice. But much as he abhorred inefficiency, he was tired of the complaints he kept hearing about the nursing home, about this and that public service being dirty or incompetent. A service was as successful as the men and women who manned it, as good as the public it catered for. People would have to demand high standards before there could be any.

He had sensed Sumer Singh's recoil, as if his surroundings were contaminating him. That species of individual might get elected—and more and more of them were coming in—but he would not have the remotest idea what election meant in terms of the service of this country. The Minister pulled his covers up to his chin. He would have liked to sleep but the nurse would come in soon to disturb him, and the meeting in the Petroleum Ministry harried his thoughts like a naked bulb he could not switch off.

Governments should use maps constantly, he thought. Had

Sumer Singh looked at the map of Asia? In his mind's eye Sardar Sahib saw it distinctly—the triangular Indian peninsula, then across the narrow slabs of Pakistan and Afghanistan, the gigantic spaces of Soviet land, beginning with the steppes, ending with Siberia. He fell into an uneasy doze, and between waking and sleeping the frontiers on the map dissolved and India and the Soviet Union lay welded together in one vast monolith. And there was a caravan, no, column of smoke, or fire, or both, travelling down the Indian plain, leaving a trail of fine ash behind it. A trail, he could see, that ran precisely along the rivers and their tributaries. Why, they are burning the Ganges, he saw in pure astonishment, even the Ganges. Now they will rewrite history and tell us the Ganges was never there. Sardar Sahib woke up chilled to find the nurse in his room.

"I dreamt our rivers were burning," he said.

"Rivers burning," she rolled her Kerala r's and giggled, "rivers don't burn."

Out in the porch Sumer Singh waited impatiently for his car to drive up. The prospect of hot coffee and an omelet with onion and chillies in it cheered him. He had become Minister of State at almost the same time that the senior Minister fell ill and had not had many encounters with the famous abrasive personality. But they always left him rattled. Now he was thinking of what the Minister did not know, that the decision had already been taken in the Cabinet a week ago after careful calculation. And there was the deal within the deal, crucial for Sumer Singh. "We do not surrender any oil . . ." the Minister had said. But the wording of the contract was vague and it was not in the public interest to disclose all the details when the resources of a border region were involved. The Cabinet had already decided that.

11

"Inheritance," Sumer Singh heard his father say as he walked into his suite at the Imperial that evening, "is sure to be scrapped."

There was an assortment of callers in the drawing room. Aunty This and Uncle That, a tray loaded with eats, and the doddering valet as well as the hotel bearer hovering over it.

"Ah," said his father, "here comes one of the minor signatories to our Government's policies."

Sumer Singh ignored the taunt. Minor! He would have to be dictator of five continents before his father would realize he counted. He smiled. Patience, he counselled himself. One of these days this old man would be dead and gone and that would be the end of that problem. These *bodies*, he thought contemptuously, creaking old carcasses sitting around holding court over cream cakes in their fool's paradise of loose talk. As if it *mattered* what they had to say. The old angered him. These were the fringes of society, along with the sick and the young, who had no contribution to make, who must be carted along like unprofitable baggage. He greeted his father and the others with graceful formality and took the cup of tea offered. Why had he come? Because the past, with its parental authority, its filial obedience, its full quota of trash, had claws of steel impossible to unclasp, however despised. They dug in and one did not dare break away. They would only go when the whole Indian past went, dismembered and ground to fine dust—so that never again could the sneer on his father's face remind him of his inadequacies.

"So—what is the word on inheritance?" his father continued.

"I am not the Government, father."

"So you aren't. One gets rather carried away by the rumours one hears."

Why did the old devil talk like that? Was he informed, or being his usual sarcastic self? Sumer Singh knew very well what the rumours about him were. Unwillingly he remembered what an English model he had slept with about the time of his staggering election victory had told him.

"It's really got you, hasn't it?" she had said shrewdly. "I can tell."

He had been thrilled beyond words with his success, but annoyed that it showed.

"Oh I know what it does," she went on.

"Yes?" He was not particularly interested in her chatter.

"There I was, never giving a damn about clothes—I was a teacher, believe it or not, and never wanted to be anything else—and then I won this beauty competition and it turned into a modelling career. And of course it wasn't just a change of work, it put me down in a different medium. It's dangerous, Sumer. Before I knew it I was thinking, I am a flawless, fabulous, priceless goddess."

"You are," agreed Sumer Singh, warm and replete with her white and gold perfection. "It shows you become what you think."

"What does that make you?" she asked.

What did that make him? He lay with his hands under his head, his eyes on the ceiling, lost in the dream. What did they know about it, the people who talked of power as though it were a tool or a load of ammunition, something external to be used? It wasn't. He had just encountered it and already he knew it could become the liquid in one's veins. It could drive out every feeling of inadequacy one had ever had, reduce every relationship to a trifle. When power possessed one everything was dispensable. He felt exalted and exultant. Power was being touched by fiery angels. Policies, programmes moved outside it. Those were the tools. Power was the goad within.

"Thinking it over, are you Sumer?"

She was lounging naked against pillows, wriggling her toes, puffing smoke out of her nostrils, but at that moment he hardly knew she was there.

"I'd swear you're going to be important," she said idly. "Oh, once you've got rid of your little complexes."

He said warily, "I beg your pardon?"

"You're too hell-bent. Dead-on, you know, even in bed."

Sumer Singh got up abruptly. The bitch didn't know

when to stop talking.

"Sex is for two people," she chatted. "Remember? Or maybe it's different over here. Just for the man. Anyway, I could make a few useful suggestions."

He dressed while rage boiled up in him, willing her to shut her mouth. He wanted to hit her face.

"What are you missing?" she enquired lazily. "In life, I mean, that you're trying to make up for? How's that for psycho-analysis?"

He tied his shoe laces and straightened up to face her, hatred in his heart. He wished he could order her from the room, but it was her room. He had left without ceremony and let her think what she liked.

One of the aunties asked fondly after the children and Sumer Singh began to give her news of them. A harmless old creature she was. He didn't mind her. But there was his father in the room, a satanic presence cutting him down. Without ever saying a word, cutting him down. Sumer Singh forced himself to look at his father and was momentarily taken aback. Shockingly old he looked this time. He remembered the other reason why he had come and would keep coming as long as his parent lived. Politics had made him even more cravenly dependent for finances on his father than before.

The tea tray was being taken away when his father said, "That was not an empty question, Sumer."

Sumer tried to make the question fit like any ordinary remark into the conversation. It was not easy with those penetrating eyes on him. His one clutching fear was that he might be disinherited.

He said hesitantly, "I don't remember."

"Inheritance, inheritance. What is going to be the trend?"

"No change from what it is, I expect. Probably heavier

taxation. It *is* a socialist Government."

"It has been for twenty-five years. It is somewhat different today. That is why I am asking." Bored with the topic his father said lightly, malevolently, "Unless of course it does not matter if I leave my money to a cats' home."

Sumer Singh felt hot and cold. Policy could not be revealed and yet the money must not be lost. His father's fortune was enormous. And he would need access to large sums soon, very soon if there was trouble over the oil deal in Parliament. Even his position in the Party would be safer if he could rely on comfortable funds. He was as yet unsure of his own standing and support. He would have to build it up with his own effort and depend on his own resources and eventually the money might be a crucial deciding factor. There was very little now that stood between him and real power, except money.

"The money is yours to do with as you choose, Sir."

"It was—until you and your new-fangled radicals rode in. Now I don't know. I wouldn't put seizure past them."

"Seizure?"

"Of stocks and shares—outright confiscation."

"That would go against the Constitution," Sumer Singh pointed out.

The sneer that substituted for a smile in his father's exchanges with him reappeared. "And who says the Constitution is a stumbling block to highway robbery?"

The hotel bearer was going in and out cleaning ashtrays and replacing them, wiping tables. Sumer Singh suppressed the tart instruction that rose to his lips to keep out of the room. It would have sounded strange, even apart from the fact that the suite was not his. All his life servants and members of the family had gone in and out of rooms, freely and casually. Doors had been left open and what a lot of doors Indian houses had. Nobody ever bothered to shut one. There was no need. Family matters were shared with everyone living under the same roof. And national matters were many times removed from family. How could there be secrecy surrounding them? But policy loudly criticized in front of servants made Sumer Singh ill at ease. He wondered if his father did it to embarrass him.

"All right," said his father briskly. "I am here this time to make some arrangements. I have decided to transfer your inheritance to you in instalments to save as much gifts tax as possible, starting immediately with the first instalment, the other two to follow if your robber Government has not swallowed it meanwhile. A lot will still be wasted in gifts tax but this is the only way I can be reasonably sure it will come to you."

It caught Sumer Singh unprepared. His senses reeled. The fervent prayers, the docile son-to-father routine, putting up with insults, *waiting*, the sheer wild agonized *waiting*—and here it was, manna from the heavens, drizzling into his lap. There must be something he had not understood in the deal.

"I'm deeply grateful, father."

"You seem certain then that it will come to you and not be wiped out in some kind of unceremonious takeover."

His father was studying him minutely, but this was not the usual cat and mouse game. There was noticeable worry and could it be—yearning? Sumer Singh was too amazed at his windfall to diagnose it. It had come without a hint on his part about what the future held.

"Frankly, I don't know, sir. It's probably just talk. You know how people talk."

"I have never known people in the market place to just talk. However, the money is now your problem, or will be shortly."

Sumer's father was astounded at himself. He had long planned to give the money in charity. The papers were ready for his signature. He could not understand what had changed his mind, except that it was beyond him when it came to the actual deed to disinherit his late-born and only son. Custom, ancestral memory and all his instincts revolted. He could not have done it had Sumer been twice as unreliable as he believed him to be. If there was a taint in his son, only providence or a miracle would put it right. He himself could not go against the ancient law of inheritance.

On the way through the corridor, Sumer Singh's attention was caught by a jeweller's window display. A weighty pendant of sapphires and rubies on a double strand of matched pearls. He had seen a woman in the Zodiac Room the other evening wearing one something like it. She had had the figure for it, dark, lush and bold. He wondered if he was coming to the end of Pixie.

In his car he thought briefly about his father's gesture and dismissed it as an eccentricity. A marvellously timely one, for not even Sumer Singh knew precisely how soon the avalanche would wipe out inheritance. He only knew that time was short.

12

On full moon nights they did not floodlight the dome of Safdarjung's tomb. The massive brass-studded doors were left open and Simrit and Raj walked through them. Just inside the dark interior where horses must have stood stamping their hooves, the musty smell of bats and old places came to them. And then they came out into the shock of full florid moonlight. It lay like a solid mass down the broad cypress-lined avenue leading to the tomb, making the trees look solemn and blue and theatrical. The pavilions and towers surrounding the central mausoleum were deeply shadowed, and the tanks, one on each side of it, dry.

"Look at that moon lording it as if it ruled the world," said Simrit. "That's how Brij feels when he goes to his father's office. The power and the glory."

"Has he said so?"

"No never. But I know it changes him. I can see it when he walks into my room on his return."

She was rather like the moon herself, he thought, obedient to rhythms she herself did not understand, satisfied that some power outside her controlled it all. Not God or any rational conception. Just fate.

"I hope you've explained the Consent Terms to Brij," said Raj.

She replied after a minute, "I was planning to. But Som must have explained them to him the other day, because by the time I'd made up my mind to talk to him, he said he didn't want to get, 'mixed up' with them. So I didn't say anything."

Raj stopped and swore in annoyance, "Why did you leave it so long? And you should have talked to him anyway. Even storming and screaming would make more sense to a child than what you do."

No wonder Som was more real, all real, even his demoniac Consent Terms. How could anyone grasp a shadow and know what to make of it, even if it was one's own mother? Restraint might be a hallmark of high breeding but it was certainly the end of vitality.

"Poor Brij," said Raj. "Poor devil."

The benches on the grass looked chalky in the matt white light. They walked over and sat down on one.

"What was Som like?" asked Raj.

"What does it matter now?"

"But what was he like?"

"He's — vivid."

"And cruel," said Raj.

"No!"

"But this document is cruel."

"That was his anger and his vanity, don't you see?"

"It's all right then to kill in anger or vanity," Raj declared.

Simrit sighed. "I don't think Som intended to do that. First of all he never believed I'd leave. And then he got carried away trying to punish me. It is possible. You slap somebody's face and that's as far as you mean to go, but you get carried away and suddenly you're involved in an orgy of violence."

"What an impressive defence you draw up," said Raj dryly. "I wish you could be as charitable to yourself."

"How can I when I'm guilty?"

"Of what, Simrit?"

"Of leaving Som. Oh not actually. He insisted on it. But I left him in spirit before that. I feel I've offended against something old and — ordained."

"People are meant to feel like that when they break men's laws," said Raj. "It's a deterrent to breaking them."

He wondered if belonging to a body that made laws, like Parliament, made one lose one's awe of them. Laws were made, not ordained.

"And then I don't know how I took clothes out of cupboards and books out of shelves and packed them into boxes and actually *left*. Such a freak wild thing to do. I don't know anybody else who would have done it."

"Simrit, you left because Som would not let you stay. After that he stuck a barbarous document on you which, if he has his fully intentioned way, will wipe whatever you earn off the map. What about *his* guilt?"

"Yes," she said without conviction, "there's that."

What in God's name became of facts in emotional crises, he wondered. Her past had a remorseless way of recalling itself in dignity, in reason, as if she herself were entirely to blame for upsetting a cosmic harmony. He could go round and round in circles with her about it. Why didn't he let her burn at the stake if martyrdom was what she wanted? Yet apart from his concern for Simrit it was a monstrous situation. It could not be tolerated. And because of it he kept trying to get some clue to Som. The Consent Terms looked more and more like an outgrowth of Som's personality as wars and treaties reflected the personalities of the statesmen who made them. The Consent Terms, he decided, were a sort of Hiroshima. But in this entire tortuous affair of her taxes there must be some very simple obvious way out. He knew what he would do.

He would call on Som and get the measure of the man. They would have a drink together and talk matters over. Two men face to face could talk most matters over and in Raj's experience there were few things that could not be talked about. One never brought them to an impasse where they couldn't.

"Why don't I go and see Som and discuss this with him?" he suggested.

"Are you mad?"

"What's wrong with it?"

"He'd never see you, once he knew it was connected with me."

"He can't be as impossible as that."

"Of course he can. He's so like Lalli temperamentally and Lalli shot his wife. Well Som's shot me — or condemned me to hard labour for a hundred years — same thing — and as far as he's concerned that's the end of it."

"Why, may I ask, did Lalli—whoever he may be—shoot his wife?"

Simrit told him.

"And where is Lalli now?"

"I don't know. I've been out of touch with him for years. He must be living in his house in Maharani Bagh. I saw him after an age when I was out with the children one day and he came and put an arm around me in the same old way and called me Bhabi. He was so completely baffled about Som leaving him, I could hardly bear the expression on his face. It was so hurt. I never thought I'd feel sorry for a man who'd shot his wife."

"You spend a lot of time feeling sorry for Som, too," Raj pointed out. "I'd say it's a waste of time."

"Yes but imagine the grotesqueness of a life where everything is new all the time. Nothing is allowed to gather a speck of dust or time or age. A life like brilliantly white false teeth perpetually on display."

"Sounds a nightmare," Raj agreed.

"And he's shut himself up in it."

"There's nothing to prevent him walking out."

"Except his whole self," said Simrit.

"I don't think that's why you feel sorry for him."

"No," she said and sank into her memories, into her past, away from him.

What did he, so determinedly free, want with this statue so hopelessly embedded in her past? But he wanted her. And in his anxiety not to inflict one more will on her, to leave her to decide, he began to talk about a new life for her as if it were a sapling, something separate to be planted and watered. Or like Safdarjung's tomb to be enjoyed by moonlight. And strangest of all, as if her new life had nothing to do with him or any man. She could be that rarity, a woman with a profession, an independent person living her own life. She didn't need a man for identity or status. There was an intensely private rapture in making and shaping one's own life that few people recognized. Raj went on talking almost to himself. He took out a cigarette, lighted it, smoked it and threw it away.

"Ready to go?" he asked.

"Yes."

The Corpus, he thought, as they walked back to the entrance, might be Simrit's tax monster. To him it looked more and more the mirror of a whole culture, people — especially women — forever taking things lying down.

13

Delhi was sprouting multi-storey buildings, a fact of modern life Raj regretted. N. N. Shah's office was in the newest of these, in one of the blocks up the road opposite Western Court and the Imperial Hotel. The road bustled with commerce, sidewalk shops of Tibetan ware, cheek by jowl with the tight-packed Janpath stalls. Cloth from Banaras brocade to nylon, and everything else under the sun — toothbrushes, brassieres, shoes, tinsel and toys. Raj stood in the entrance of Shah's block looking up and down the street with its thick tangle of traffic. At nine-thirty in the morning the day was still dust- free, but not for long. Swirling, stinging dust in summer, dust and thunder in the rains, fine pervasive dust now in winter—dust was a year-round presence in Delhi.

He went into the building, found Shah's Company listed on the brand new brass plate in the wall and took the lift up. He had telephoned the secretary for an appointment but Shah had come on the line himself and with his usual punctilious courtesy had made an appointment for this morning. The papers concerning Simrit's son's inheritance clipped together in the file he was carrying, Raj was aware of the dividends of the very different legacy his father had left him. There were at least two strong continuous examples of it—Ram Krishan, a close friend on whom Raj could always rely, and unexpectedly, Shah. The first time they had met, Shah had said, "Our fathers knew each other, Mr Garg."

"I didn't know," admitted Raj.

"Your father helped mine with a difficult contract, quite a crucial one for him, and would take nothing in return. My father spoke of Mr Garg with the greatest respect and affection. I remember him telling stories about a government officer most unusual for his time. When others were worrying about their dignity, he said, here was one quite indifferent to his, wearing shorts to work, going about on a bicycle instead of by car, dining at the homes of his juniors, and his own house open to one and all."

It was the kind of legacy that survived taxation, Raj had replied, making Shah laugh, but Shah had added seriously, "Much has changed in our country, Mr Garg. I remember a time when big deals could be put through on the telephone, only by word of mouth and reputation, and they were honoured. That no longer happens. The atmosphere is altogether different now. But one thing that does still matter to people like me is family contacts. If there is anything I can do for you, it will be my pleasure."

Mr Shah had proceeded to invite Raj to parties, to send him fruit and a bottle of Scotch at Christmas, and pleasantly enquire after him at intervals for no reason at all. Raj had done nothing for him in return but be friendly. And he had finally taken advantage of Shah's repeated offer to be of assistance when he had decided to stand for election to Parliament three years earlier. Raj had gone to him then to ask for funds and Shah had immediately agreed to contribute the money and put his organization at Raj's disposal as well.

"You haven't even asked me what ticket I'm standing on," Raj had protested.

"I have much to ask you but those are details. Let us settle the main business first."

"Suppose I told you I was standing on the Communist ticket," Raj baited him.

Shah's antipathy to Communism was almost as active as his yearning for Japan.

He lapsed into silence. Then he said thoughtfully, "In my opinion, Mr Garg, a man's morality must sometimes be judged by his character and his motive, not always his action. If you stood on the Communist ticket, I would try to understand why."

"And what would you decide in the end?" persisted Raj.

"You put me in a quandary," admitted Shah, with his good-humoured chuckle.

"Well I'm standing as an Independent," said Raj. "I look upon it as a failure among us. The country should offer something definite that an educated man can commit himself to."

Shah had helped generously. He told Raj he considered it a repayment of his father's debt to Raj's father. When Raj later wondered how much he owed his success to Shah's money and expert organization, Shah blandly remarked that that was a question no one could answer, even in business.

"In any case," said Shah, "you are a good man to back. I don't mean a winner, but that good men are rare in politics. I am glad I could be of help."

The conversation came back to Raj as he was ushered into the office by a smiling secretary and Shah rose to greet him. He came round his desk and offered Raj one of the armchairs on the other side of the room. He took the other himself and rang the bell for coffee.

"I won't join you," he said. "You know I don't drink coffee or tea."

The smooth round face looked twenty years younger than his age, which Raj knew was forty-four. It bespoke a life of unbroken habit, plain diet and abstemiousness. Raj was intrigued by the thought of where such people got their kicks. But Shah, usually genial, was downcast this morning.

"You don't look your cheerful self," said Raj.

"Is there something to look cheerful about?" his host enquired. "This is the time of year we normally interview candidates for selection. But we can't fill all our vacancies or expand as we are equipped to, because Government is anti-expansion. But you have come to talk about something else."

"I don't understand," said Raj, "why industry hasn't got together and put its view before the Government, made a firm united stand."

"You must be joking, Mr Garg. Even our donations go on—under cover, of course. They have to. I have personally given five lakhs last month."

"Even you?" Raj was incredulous.

Shah looked dejected. "What alternative is there? But tell me about your problem."

The problem languished in Raj's mind. The important question, still unanswered, kept surfacing. What did people ike Shah or Simrit believe in? What, if anything, would they fight to defend? The incongruity of bringing Simrit's problem to Shah hit him as forcefully as a physical blow. People who believed in fate should be left to fate, he thought grimly. He himself belonged to a thinking, acting breed, one that would not settle for what fate dumped in its lap.

Shah said, "If you've finished your coffee, I will ask our legal adviser to come in. I told him you wanted to consult him on a private matter. I am sure you would prefer to see him alone."

"Actually," said Raj, "this is a case that should have publicity. It concerns my friend, Mrs Raman, who was at your party the other evening. She is in great distress over the tax aspect of the financial settlement at her divorce."

"Really? But her husband is a very wealthy man, and I understood—you know how people talk—that he has made a very generous settlement."

"That doesn't quite rhyme with the facts," said Raj. "It's an extravagant settlement on paper—for the children, or rather the boy. For her it's murder."

Shah's face cleared. "Then it does provide for the children."

"For the boy primarily, and the leftovers for the girls."

"That is quite natural," Shah assured him.

"Well all right. It's not that part of it we want to change. It's the part that puts the whole tax burden on Mrs Raman though she gets nothing out of the fortune in her name."

"But you said, did you not, that it goes to her son?"

Raj said, "But Mrs Raman is stuck with the taxes till it goes to her son and that is not till he's twenty-five."

"A wise measure," said Shah. "I know of cases where immature young men have blown up fortunes. Even twenty-five is too young to inherit a large sum of money."

Now which way do I hang up this bloody problem so that the blood shows, thought Raj. The woman angle make about as much dent as an insect on a laser beam. The Republic of India has passed many laws, Simrit my love, but people like N. N. Shah live in it, friendly, God-fearing fellows who wouldn't harm a fly but who can't for the life them see when a woman is bleeding to death with taxes.

"This fortune in Mrs Raman's name must have been there for years," said Shah. "I mean it was not put there at the time of the divorce."

"No, of course not," said Raj.

"Then it was part of the financial arrangement during their marriage," Shah deduced. "A good arrangement for a married couple."

"Only they aren't married any more," said Raj dryly.

"But divorce is not part of our tradition," Shah pointed out. "It is rare. Arrangements made to last during a marriage do not, after all, provide for the possibility of divorce. And so this arrangement was left as it was for convenience sake."

"The divorce," said Raj laboriously, "is a fact. It has taken place."

"Yes indeed. It is very sad," said Shah. "Well I will call our legal adviser in. You had better leave those papers with him."

Raj came out of Shah's office and stood in the low arched entrance. Across the road to the right, in front of a stall selling bolts of silk and brocade, he had accosted Shaila months after she had left him. She had recoiled as if he had slapped her. That, more than their brief exchange, had stung him, making him rough and peremptory when what he had wanted was to plead.

"You haven't answered the telephone or my letters."

"It was better not to."

"Come and have a cup of coffee with me now, Shaila.

We've got to talk this over."

"There's nothing to talk over."

She turned to go and he grasped her arm.

Shaila said tensely, "You're making a scene."

Complete cold conviction had settled in him that he could never reach her again. And he knew he would no longer try. A woman who could deny plain fact might well drive him, even if he could win her, into the realms of insanity. He had once and for all let her go. But here he was, he thought wryly, part of a culture that could and did do the same, and that harboured great illusions as if they were facts. The situation was not without humour—if enough people would laugh.

A passing taxi slowed for him but he waved it on. He decided to walk, to clear his head of the figures of Simrit's tax case. Once again he had been lifted completely out of the simple arithmetic of his own much more austere existence. Was it only that morning he had looked at his bank statement lying open among other papers on his desk, with the fine spidery handwriting showing he had nine hundred rupees in his current account? He had felt quite elated at the manageability of the amount. Simrit's case, after a while, became a string of zeros. But the session with Shah's lawyer had pushed his own affairs to the background again and Simrit's complications had come streaming back.

The whole idea—whoever paid the taxes on it—was fantasy when so many still lived tortured lives. Six lakhs! Not for use—for education or more comfortable living—but merely to be left to accumulate, to grow huge and bloated, as Simrit put it, until the boy was twentyfive! There is actually a man here in Delhi who drew up this fantastic arrangement, he reminded himself. He frequently had to remind himself of the actuality of Som. There are men, he thought, whose minds work in this way. This is the psychology we have to contend with, the outlook that will lead to the destruction here in India, not of particular targets, but of life as we have known it till now. Even my own modest affluence will not last. For how could even his own standards, each earned, survive the temper of the times balancing now on the razor's edge between reason and violence? So far there had been only isolated shots fired at money, privilege, prestige. But if the heavy artillery gathered, as it would, not only would the rich with their riches be wiped out but the growing struggling middle classes as well. And how could it be otherwise when there were men like the one who had drawn up the Consent Terms?

Raj quickened his pace. He had to be in his seat in the Lok Sabha at eleven o'clock. A few days ago Sumer Singh's acceptance of the Soviet oil exploration offer had sparked anxious questions in the House rising to a furor, as if the general tension of the days and weeks before the decision had finally snapped, breaking into loud, irregular cries of alarm. Members had demanded that the Soviet contract be laid on the table of the House. The Minister of State had argued it was not in the public interest to reveal the details. And Raj had found himself on his feet waiting for the commotion to die down, to catch the Speaker's eye and to say that Parliament had a right to documents and information. Today, after the debate the offer would be voted on. An unusual case for Parliament, and an uneasy situation.

14

There was a serenity about the beautifully proportioned, circular, colonnaded building where the two Houses of Parliament met, a calm looking place enshrining the rule of law. But for some time now it had contained more fever than calm. The Speaker's voice could hardly be heard when sittings broke into pandemonium. Here the Constituent Assembly had met in 1946 to proclaim India an independent socialist republic, an emotional event in the language of the first Prime Minister: "I do feel," he had said, "there is a magic in the moment of transition from the old to the new, something of that magic which one sees when the night turns into day, and even though the day may be a cloudy one, it is day after all..." Freedom and daybreak. Freedom carrying the cross of Partition. But freedom. Daybreak then, thought Raj, but where are we heading now?

He walked up the stairs and stood in the wide curving corridor looking through an entrance at the sunlit courtyard dividing the two Houses of Parliament. Simrit's problem, now in the hands of Shah's competent lawyer, was still at the back of his mind. He determinedly cleared his head of it. It was unwise to enter the Lok Sabha in a contemplative mood, especially on a day of debate and decision, though the voting on the oil exploration offer would not take place till afternoon or evening, after the debate. This was a place of business, enacted among men and women who were not all Parliamentarians by conviction or temperament. Some were openly committed to overthrow Parliament and the Constitution by fair means or foul. Many imagined the world would be a better place as soon as privilege and good taste had been driven out of it. Raj had to admit some sympathy for this latter view—though it was not comforts he minded but the fact that they seemed to make people insensitive. I wonder, he thought with a rush of affection for this building and the contradictions it housed, if there is another Parliament quite like ours, quite so much up against the possibility of its own demise, quite so aspiring in the face of so many problems. This was and could not be anything but an Indian assembly—a microcosm of all the growth and decay, the hope and despair of India—its brave modernity along with its gross old superstitions. Parliament carried them all and tried to turn them to good account. Raj had a fanatic's devotion to Parliament. As an outsider, a non-belonger to any party, he knew that what he belonged to was the Constitution, the laws, the whole intangible edifice constructed at "daybreak."

ndia—his India—was that. If anything happens to Parliament, if it goes, he thought, I and people like me—the different ones, the minorities, the ones who don't disappear obligingly into the mass—will go to the dungheap. We won't count. And all these thoughts fused these days into what Raj would have called prayer had he admitted to praying.

He could not explain the queer unease that had hold of him. He raised a hand in greeting, smiled and nodded to other MP's as he walked along the outer corridor to the chamber. The stone staircase on the left leading to the visitors' gallery was almost festive with people going up. It promised to be a full house and a lively debate.

His discomfort mounted as he noticed canvassing in full swing in the Central Hall and the lobbies. Since his own entry into Parliament three years earlier, the role of an Independent had begun to matter more. A small, inconsequential group before, who could vote one way or another and not make much difference to the result, now each was sought out and wooed. The Government, since the recent split in its own party, needed every vote it could get and the scene in the lobbies before a major debate could look like the Stock Exchange on market day. It was anybody's guess how many would hold on to their principles in an auction where the stakes were high and sometimes dazzling. Raj stood detachedly in a corner watching. This was democracy at work—a chaotic, inept system of government, especially for India—until you thought of other systems.

He took his seat in the chamber and nodded to a colleague across the aisle. Sumer Singh walked in and went to the Treasury Benches on the other side of the room. Raj noticed the slip from Sumer Singh on his own desk asking if he would see him in his office during the lunch break. It said the Minister of State would take only a few minutes of his time.

Sumer Singh began his speech. It was not hard to be an effective speaker in the high-domed room. The acoustics were good, the mikes helped but there was never complete silence. Sumer Singh, however, soon had the assembly's attention. He had a loud clear voice and he knew how to use it. He even managed to make the technicalities of oil exploration interesting, and he was going right back to the start, tracing India's efforts since independence, explaining the steps Sardar Sahib had taken to get things going. At mention of the old Minister's name there was a burst of spontaneous clapping and table-thumping. The old man was an all-India figure, an institution, and admiration for him was warm and generous. Raj heard Sumer Singh announce, "In the light of our own experience we decided to accept the Soviet offer."

But then the speech seemed to be going on as if manifest ly more than the terms of an oil exploration agreement were being proposed. Sumer Singh was giving public notice of a very different event, the shadowy beginnings of a vast alliance. He was discussing policy in general and countries who would figure in it. He even spoke of the Indian Ocean and what the new alliance would mean in trade and protection to its waters. He was inviting the assembly, he said in conclusion, "to look in a new direction." And he asked the House to cast its vote for the new direction by accepting the Soviet offer.

Raj left the chamber deeply disturbed. Sumer Singh was in his office. He apologized for asking Raj to come.

"But please consider it a measure of your own influence among the Independents," he said with charming sincerity. "We want to be sure of your support in the vote."

Raj took a chair.

"The Independents have two fears about this agreement," he said bluntly.

He had no idea how the other forty in the group had reacted. There had not been time to find out. But since he
had been singled out as their spokesman he might as well get
his own doubts clear.

"One," he rapped out, "is the danger of giving exploration
in Jammu to the Soviet Union. We believe both Russia and
America should be kept out of the Kashmir region and an
uncontroversial offer accepted. It's a question after all of
buying the know-how, a straight business deal—nothing to do
with policy in general."

Sumer Singh waited, looking both pleasant and vigilant.

"Two," said Raj. "The wording of the contract is vague. It
nowhere makes it clear that we will not give up any of our
oil."

Sumer Singh took a cigarette from the box on his desk
and held the box out to Raj. Raj took one, feeling a little
ashamed of his brusqueness. He had been on edge all day.
He made an effort to unwind. After all he had wanted to
know this man. Votes contracts, politics, too often
passed in their set-up for life. Here they were face to face,
about the same age too—an opportunity not to be lost in
horse trading.

"Do you know," said Sumer Singh, "it is wonderful—
and refreshing—what a stir where has been about this oil deal.
I could feel the House bristling with it while I spoke. It's
seldom one gets that kind of all-out reaction on any subject.
One feels lucky if one gets a proper hearing. But I think I
was able to convince them the Soviet offer is best for us."

"The best offer?" demanded Raj.

"The best overall choice in our circumstances, as I explained—and with future collaborations in mind. It would tie up,
you see, with other deals we already have with them, make
them all more smooth-running. And then we can't forget

our early help came from them. I was with the Minister for a long discussion before we signed the agreement and we were talking about it."

That silenced Raj's next question, about the Minister's own reaction, but oddly it alerted him. There was something here that could not stand on its own, without a seal of approval from a universally trusted source.

Raj said more reasonably, "I still think that safety for us and for this whole region lies in no close alliance with anybody."

Sumer Singh acknowledged this. He had to, Raj thought uncharitably. Twenty years of non-alignment backed it up. It had been bungled at times, but it had been a basically sound policy. If it was going to be re-cast now it would have to be in a fluid mould that would leave room for manoeuvre.

"But that's past now," said Sumer Singh. "We have to decide where we stand. The West is in decay. They know it themselves. Look at the upheavals in Western society."

"The West has been in decay a long time," Raj observed, "but the rot has a way of falling off and the rest renews itself because people are permitted to think."

"We have all believed that," said Sumer Singh indulgently, "as students."

"On the contrary," said Raj, "most students follow Marx—and perhaps they should. Balance comes later in life."

"Those are theories. We in politics have to listen to the mass urge."

For the second time that morning Raj had the vivid impression that the world as he knew it was slipping away and some bigger outer future shaping itself remorselessly around them. There was no view through the window of Sumer Singh's office. It looked out into a section of walled verandah. Beyond it, out of Raj's line of vision lay the courtyard between the two Houses, which sunlit and serene he had contemplated before disappearing into the suspense of the debate. Now he was in a fever to get up and reassure himself that it and Parliament were still there. He and Sumer Singh, he realized, were not men of different political opinions supporting the same system. They belonged to different lines of thinking and the future of Asia would depend on which line won. He slumped back in his chair suddenly tired as the day's discomfort found its focus.

"One mass is not like another," he said almost to himself. "Ours, for instance, has built well under restrained leadership, under good men. It can again. We don't need other people's solutions."

He knew as he said it that other people's solutions could not be ignored. There they were staring one in the face with their achievements, each holding out its own reward. The West had its good society, its great glittering rich society, but for people who still had to sweat for their daily bread it was Marx who was his brother's keeper—ready with help on easy credit terms, with scientists, technicians and rupee loans. And how could any country who needed those turn its back on Marx? Maybe, after all, there was no option but to choose between Marx and anti-Marx and the party in power had chosen. But this was a gamble that allowed no retreat.

Sumer Singh smiled.

"It's easy to see why the Prime Minister has a high opinion of you. I personally endorse it. The Prime Minister is very interested in the adult literacy scheme you have started in your constituency. He asked me to tell you he would be glad to contribute to it from his own special Fund. And apart from that, he has been wanting to talk to you about whether you'd consider tearing yourself away from the constituency and serving abroad."

And vacating the constituency for another of their yes-men, thought Raj. No I would not. Not for the plummiest assignment in the cushiest post. You don't get rid of me so fast.

Aloud he said, "I'm afraid I'm not cut out for the diplomatic life. I feel I have a job to do here."

He got up and pushed his chair back abruptly. He was wasting his time when there was none to lose. He would have to hurry if he was to round up the others in his group and tell them of his urgent belief that they must vote against the Soviet offer. Sumer continued affable and saw him to the door with a smile, but when the door shut behind him Raj was certain his name and face had been duly noted, and no more invitations or opportunities would come his way. Maybe even Shah, with his donations to policies he didn't believe in, would fade out of his life. The sun would be rising in a different direction and it would be very chilly for those outside its orbit.

Three hours later, when the Soviet offer won the majority vote, Raj, watching the results flashed by computer, thought with a sombre detachment, well, that's democracy—the victory of numbers—and like progress it doesn't always do the right thing.

Simrit stood unsmiling on the steps as he came out of Parliament. They walked down the steps in silence, waves of talk and excitement breaking round them. On the bottom step she put an arm sympathetically through his. Raj waved his free hand in greeting to the Members of Parliament getting into their cars and others walking out to the bus stop. Ahead in Vijay Chowk men and women on foot and on cycles, released from their offices, streamed past. Behind them cars were beginning to drive out of Parliament. The blue haze of evening was vanishing into darkness.

"I didn't know you were in the House," said Raj.

"I had to hear the debate. Joshi got me a pass. All that talk of alliance and a new direction was frightening. What's going to happen now?"

"That is what I want to know from you, from all these people walking down the road, and from everyone else in the country. Because the ones like me are too few to do anything alone. Have you got time for a cup of coffee or do you have to get home to your litter?"

"What a word."

"That's how it hits me sometimes, all of them tugging and pulling at you. What does it leave of you?"

"I'll make you a cup of coffee at home," she offered. "wouldn't that be better than sitting in a restaurant?"

"It would—without your litter. All right, let's go. With you I face a dead end at every turn, unlike Som who must have ridden roughshod and triumphant. Did he?"

"I suppose so. I mean I didn't think so at the time. We were married."

"You were married." he repeated. "Amen."

She took his hand in the taxi. It had an unexpected vibrancy and warmth. Raj deliberately withdrew his. No hand-holding games with her. No games of any sort. With her it had to be on a long, strong basis. Simrit's look was warm and understanding. One of these days, thought Raj, when we're not talking about her infernal taxes, we'll have to get down to each other. But that couldn't be bungled.

The litter, he was glad to find, was dispersed in various rooms, mostly in Brij's terrace room judging from the music and noise coming from it. Occasionally it announced its presence by a thudding up and down the stairs. Simrit walking in and out with a tray and cups had a soft domestic sparkle about her.

"Stop fidgeting, Raj. Sit down, I'm bringing you some

coffee as fast as I can."

Her hair in the reddish lamplight looked more bronze than black and her body oddly lacked the fullness of women who had had children. Was it possible there were depths in her, uncommitted, even untouched? Had her life with Som, tumultuous of a kind—with its pageantry and symbols—absorbed only the surfaces? He discarded the thought. There was nothing surface about the hold Som still had on her imagination. The marriage clung to her vitals. He was intensely aware of her as she sat on the carpet near his chair looking at him for answers, as people always were, hanging on to what he said, mesmerized by it. It was a power he would happily have dispensed with at this moment in return for plain animal attraction.

"What is going to happen, Raj?"

"I don't know any more. But I'm afraid that between Marx and anti-Marx what India stands for may get drowned out in the confusion."

How passionately we hold on to India's special destiny, he thought, those of us who believe in it, to a future that must arise out of her own past and no other, preserving all her own essence. And we keep taking for granted the special protection of the Almighty for all eternity. Simrit, for instance, goes to sleep every night believing everything will be exactly the same and exactly as safe in the morning for no better reason than that "this is India."

"To hell with it all," he said suddenly. "You know, Simrit, I talk too much. You are sitting there now waiting for me to talk, to expound."

"What's wrong with that?"

"Nothing. Except that if I were a hunchback or a dwarf I doubt if anyone would notice it once I started talking."

"But isn't that wonderful!" she said.

"It's a curse. No one—no woman ever says: What a *man* this is. No one falls in love with *me*, they fall in love with my mind. What first struck you about me?"

"Well—" she looked guilty.

"You came into my garden that day to hear me *talk*. And the hitch about talk is it doesn't get into a woman's vitals the way actions do, or even the crudest kind of physical relationship. Even a man who slaps her around is more of a reality."

"What nonsense," said Simrit unexpectedly.

"You mean it does?

"It's a crying need, as much as anything is," said Simrit. "I used to get quite desperate for it. And if I'd known you well before my divorce, there might not have been any divorce. Knowing you would have taken care of one need and my marriage another."

"And the three of us would have lived happily together," said Raj. "That was just what I meant. I'm a mind, not a man to the female of the species."

Brij came in trailed by younger members of the litter.

"Isn't it time for dinner?" he looked directly at his mother.

There was a hint of impatience about him. I've been young with an appetite for dinner too, thought Raj, but more cordial about it, not as if it were my right. He wondered what it was about the boy that failed to draw him. A handsome lively youngster, but in an odd unyouthful way engrossed in his comforts. He was young and there was time to change, but it would take something more to kindle this one, and it might already be too late.

"I hadn't noticed the time," said Simrit. "Stay for dinner, Raj."

The time, Raj checked his watch, was not very late. She could have asked the children to wait a little. But she was accustomed to obeying them. He thought of staying on and grappling conversationally with the boy, but decided against it. The boy was civil, good-humoured and closed. And, Raj guessed, most things were outside the rim of his involvement.

Simrit walked downstairs with Raj, then up again slowly. The younger ones were getting rowdy as they waited for dinner with Brij inventing games for them. What an idiot Raj is, for all his mind, she thought. After all attraction had to start somewhere and what better starting point than the mind? From there the journey was infinite. She was astir now with many kinds of awareness, beginning of all things with his beauty, the long-limbed fluid grace where no gesture was ever forced, the ease and range of movement that came of walking, speaking and living with open naturalness. If she had ever doubted that she loved him she could not any longer.

15

"We can't use this article, Raj."

Raj almost fainted every time he entered Ram Krishan's
office. The room was hermetically sealed, with not a crack
or a crevice to let in air and both bars of the heater were on.
When Ram Krishan went out he wrapped a woollen scarf
around his head. Knitted wool socks — no readymade synthetic
stuff for him — kept his feet snug. Baggy suited and unbrushed,
he was the most atrociously dressed individual Raj knew and
one of the best of men. He had been untidy enough before
but had become impossibly so since the death of his wife
two years earlier. And Raj had never known anyone who
felt so cold. This, too, seemed to increase with her loss, as

though his world had become a frozen wilderness without her warmth. He never spoke of her. Since the day Raj had stood beside him as he committed her ashes to the Ganges at Hardwar, Ram Krishan had never once mentioned Vinita's name and everything about him had sagged and drooped.

"May I open your window a mite?" Raj asked hopefully.

"No you may not. The temperature is eighteen degrees today."

"Centigrade," Raj pointed out. "And it's above, not below zero. And we're not in the Arctic zone. Think what happens to Indians who migrate to Canada."

"They deserve what they get. Don't argue, and sit down— if you're staying."

Raj complied, turning the chair around and sitting astride it with his arms along the top. Ram Krishan looked up, took off his glasses and sighed.

"Turn it around. Why can't you sit in a chair the right way round?" Raj obliged

"Why can't you use my article?" he asked pleasantly.

"You know why. I wanted a factual article. I told you to go and get your material from Sumer Singh. He was the one who was negotiating. I would have preferred the senior Minister but he's practically on his death-bed and I'm not sure what he says goes now. Sumer Singh was the man to see and the time to do it was when the offer came up in Parliament. All this philosophy about Marx and anti-Marx we can do without. Haven't you got enough work being an M.P. without propounding theories nobody will publish?"

"I couldn't do it any earlier. I've been tied up with one or two other matters. Anyway, it's a good article," Raj insisted. "It says things we ought to be thinking about."

"Maybe it does but it's not what I want."

Ram Krishan put on his glasses, frowned down at the typed

heets on his desk and took his glasses off again.

"You should get bi-focals," said Raj helpfully.

"When I want your advice I'll ask for it. I wish you had one into Government service like your father. That would have kept you out of Parliament which obviously doesn't keep you very busy. Anyway you can take your article somewhere else. I don't want your theories about oil and psychology. There isn't enough newsprint in circulation for that. And t is not a news weekly type of article at all. Send it to a magazine. Here, take it away."

Ram Krishan pushed it aside and fidgeted with his glasses.

"You're always complaining that no one wants new ideas," said Raj equably, "that they hang on to the same old ones, whether they have any practical value or not, like socialism—whatever that might mean in our particular circumstances. Well here is a new idea. I think it is quite revolutionary to propose — in India today — that socialism is just a catchword. and that for better economics we should try some variation of it, I don't care what you call it. That's probably why the old Minister has been chucked out like an old shoe — or would be if he weren't ill and dying — because he refuses to get tied to catchwords."

"All right, all right. But I don't want your article."

Ram Krishan pulled the tray containing the morning's mail toward him and started shuffling through it. Raj loosened his tie. He got up and began to walk around the small room in the hope of circulating some air, taking care to avoid a wide radius of the heater. He went on talking.

"And they keep throwing out people who think. What are they afraid of? That people might find them appealing and get converted? Then why don't they produce a few appealing ideas of their own, ones that will work? You've always said that one can only combat an idea with another idea — not with clamps."

Ram Krishan went on shuffling through his mail.

"Never mind what I said," he muttered. "I've said too damn much all my life and you've got a memory like an elephant."

Raj looked down with a pang at his father's closest friend, sad that he could do nothing to alleviate the emptiness. During his college days he had been a constant visitor to Ram Krishan's house, the recipient, along with a generation of students, of a welcoming but absent-minded hospitality and of incisive views on life and current events. Most of his fundamental thinking had grown out of what he had first heard in that house. In those days Ram Krishan having decided not to continue his law practice, had held a lectureship at the University. Later he had got busy founding a daily newspaper. Men seemed to get involved in a lot more things then. Financial security mattered less and a full and satisfying use of one's faculties much more. There was a lot of mental energy and a great many theories about. In Ram's home the atmosphere positively crackled with them. Young men came there to argue and some to be enchanted. Ram who had never had children of his own treated every young person he knew as fully adult.

Ram Krishan looked up.

"Take it away, Raj" he said briefly. "Put it in a book or a journal — something else. Now take it away."

Ram Krishan himself had kept a quality of freshness probably because he had been protesting against one thing and another since his own university days and quite systematically since he had become owner and editor of a weekly paper. Before independence he had been outspokenly anti-British and forced to shut down his paper several times since he could not and would not pay the fines imposed. But he had gone on being anti a great many developments after Independence too, a disconcerting gadfly no one could impale on any convenient label. The Reds called him a reactionary and the conservatives a Red. He had written stormily against Partition at a time when the nation was being asked to accept the accomplished fact. He had been scathing about the Hindu Code Bill, a monumental reform, because he believed every other community should have been included in it. During the Hindi language agitation he had infuriated the Hindi zealots by declaring it was a crime to destroy any achievement and that the English language counted as an Indian achievement. For this he had had the headlights of his car smashed and copies of his paper burned in the street. Yet there remained the anomaly that his mother tongue was Hindi and he spoke it with a scholar's love for it. There had in the past been a prophetic streak in Ram Krishan. What he said sounded glaringly inobvious but sooner or later events rode it into truth. And everything he did and said had vigour. But lately he had seemed dejected and lack-lustre. It was not like him not to join issue, not take on a challenge. It worried Raj.

Raj said, "Even if my article isn't quite what you expected, it does raise some interesting points. Here you've been hitting out at everything ever since I've known you—"

"Naturally," said Ram Krishan dryly. "It was my job, as you just said, to produce ideas, not to swallow facts and programmes wholesale even if the Government of our own choosing put them before us—or go to sleep over them."

"Well then what's happened now?"

"I'm old. That's what has happened. And I'm soggy with repetition, like your dying Petroleum Minister. And no one is listening to any of it. They're too befogged with their own fool theories. And I'm too old to care. Now go away. I have work to do."

It was true he had work to do. But for a long time Raj

had not seen it claim his entire concentration. To give his conscientious best to a job had been a cardinal principle, almost a natural reaction with him. Now it mattered less and less.

Raj sat down. He took out a cigarette.

"Please," said Ram Krishan, looking up.

Raj put the cigarette back. He had not had one for three hours and in this suffocating room he felt like crawling up a wall without one.

"There is something I'd like your advice about," he said.

"What?"

"It's a tax matter."

"Why come to me? Go to a tax lawyer."

"I have been to one."

Raj pondered the curious fact that one went to an expert for cold assessment and then to someone else for all the layers of possibility that finally helped in decision. There was that tender area in and around human problems that did not fit into formulas, and needed more than calculation and expertise.

"I won't take your time now," said Raj. "I can come over to the house some time. Tomorrow?"

"What? Yes. All right." Ram Krishan went on reading his mail.

"What time?"

"What?" Ram Krishan looked up, focussing with difficulty on Raj through his glasses. He took them off.

"I said what time," repeated Raj. "It's not my problem, by the way. It is someone else's. A woman I know."

"I've known men to get involved with women," said Ram, Krishan, "not with their taxes. But you come from a queer breed. Your father got involved with an idea and on the strength of it he took off from his family and his past. It is an extraordinary thing, this Christian philosophy in our particular setting. It is an incomplete philosophy, even though it has all the attractions of direct solution. But you are taking off on taxes, are you?"

Raj was silent. He had thought about the extent and depth of his "take-off." There was no avoiding it. Simrit and Simrit's problem had become a daily business. He had kept turning it over in his mind for a hint of romantic or sexual involvement. Those were there but it yielded most of all a strange necessity. It was not a question of Simrit for himself—at least not until he had some sign from her. It was Simrit for herself he wanted, Simrit to forsake her shadows and begin to live.

"It's the injustice of the thing," he said finally. "It sort of puts one into a cold fury. An objective fury."

Ram Krishan smiled faintly.

"The injustice of the thing," he repeated.

Yes, that would be the matchless kindling for the big and small fires of purpose. Raj would obviously be involved in it up to his ears.

"What brand of injustice is this?" he enquired.

Raj told him of Simrit's divorce and the tax settlement.

"It is merciless," he explained. "There is a fortune in her name in shares, put there to save the husband taxes. And her own small income will be taxed at the highest rate because of these shares. She is not earning much at the moment but if she works from now till doomsday and manages to earn a reasonable living she will hardly see a fraction of it. This settlement cripples any effort she might try to make at supporting herself or saving for her future."

"There must be other ways for the husband to save tax."

"There are. The lawyer I consulted said the obvious thing was to make a trust for the children, but that would attract gifts tax which the husband is not prepared to pay. He's prepared to let her break under the burden, though. It's butchery, the last drop of blood extracted."

It would take Suren's son, thought Ram Krishan, to see blood and tragedy in a legal document and to pit himself against it though it had nothing to do with him. He remembered the case years earlier when Suren had fanatically defended a colleague charged with supplying information to Pakistan. Suren had branded it a Dreyfus case based on cooked up evidence. It was Suren's study of the case, one that did not remotely concern him, and his intense application to detail, that had cleared the man of suspicion. And Ram suspected it was not altogether because of the evidence Suren had painstakingly unearthed. In the end his persistence had won, his sheer refusal to let an error remain on record.

"In matters like this tax problem," Ram Krishan pointed out, "sentiment and custom have almost as much to say as the law. The Hindu woman traditionally has no rights apart from what her father or her husband choose to bestow on her. The law has changed some of that, but attitudes haven't changed much, which is clear from the husband's attitude in this case and the court's acceptance of such a document. A woman can apparently still be used as a convenience for tax purposes by her husband even after he has divorced her. In any other country it would be indefensible and outrageous. No court would have looked at any document that expected a woman to pay out of her own earnings as a subsidy for her ex-husband. The whole idea would have been preposterous."

"That was my own impression," said Raj, "but of course the difficulty here is that this document is supposed to have been drawn up with her consent."

"That's just rubbish," retorted Ram Krishan. "What did

our lawyer say?"

"Lawyers just look at what the law says. And these Consent Terms have been ratified in court. As far as the law is concerned, Simrit has been effectively delivered to the hangman—with her own consent. Any reprieve is outside the province of the law, unless she fights the case. And that's out as her signature is there and she hasn't the money or the heart for a fight."

"She could of course walk away with the shares and see what happens," Ram Krishan meditated, scratching his chin, "since they are hers — legally!"

"It might solve many problems," admitted Raj. "But about the only thing she walked away with were her books, by the hundred, and her children. She's not a very practical person."

"I see," said Ram Krishan.

He sat back fingering his glasses.

"Come on Monday at six," he said suddenly. "Bring her too."

When Raj left, Ram Krishan wondered why he had added that. After Vinita's death he had withdrawn one by one the spontaneous extras — unsolicited comment, laughter for its own sake, tenderness, pleasure in the spill of morning light on his bedroom floor. He had done it with deliberation, not rancour. A love had been taken from him. He had merely arranged his life sensibly around the fact. The world continued bearable and more, but spontaneity and overflow were things that had to be shared. With her and no other. He noticed Raj's article still lying on the table and his own hand spread on it. The hand one had started life with was there to the end, while another part of one, much more united flesh of one's flesh, fell away, as if one could carry on without it.... Well, he had carried on.

He folded Raj's article and put it in a drawer. Raj look ed so much like his father and could hammer out arguments like him, too. Ram Krishan could hear his old friend talking to him out of a youthful argument long ago. They had been friends since childhood but Suren's collision with Christianity and his conversion to it had added breadth to their association spreading a multitude of data before them to look at from two points of view, his and Suren's.

Conversion had charged Suren with a new energy, irresistible in its vigour. We're the same age, Ram Krishan had often thought, but how young he is, striding around like a prince in his new-found empire of the spirit. The ancient society they both lived in, the society that prescribed the rules and behaviour of man all the days of his life, had no hold on Suren any more. The two of them had talked, argued, quarrelled with a wholeness Ram Krishan had not been able to summon since. His chief regret was that at that age the advantage had been with Suren, with his new discovery, his passionate, wholly occupying convert's love for it, and the involvement that swept him with it. Ram Krishan himself had remained somewhat of a spectator, envious at times, never entirely convinced but always caught up and carried along. Later, much later after Suren's death, he had found flaws in Suren's thesis, and through those at last a ripe contribution of his own to make to their common theme, but by then it was too late.

"Here society still respects a man for giving up the world," he could hear Suren saying, "for turning his back on desire. Oh, I can understand renunciation. It is a hankering, and a noble one, in the human process. But there are times when it is wrong. If your right hand gets gangrene and you cut it off, you are removing disease. But if your right hand slaps a man in temper or commits a crime, cutting it off is not the answer because a hand with capacity can be used for the good. So you can't simply make a virtue of renunciation as Hinduism does. That's what defeats this country. It makes a man draw back and do nothing in a situation when he should take more responsibility, face up to things and stand firm."

Ram Krishan reflected now that he himself had not renounced anything, nor had he wanted to. He had merely gone on living in an altered key, accepting the inexorable logic of death. Logic was another theme that had come under Suren's fire. Friendship, love, he had declared, the whole gamut of emotional relationship, the very idea of giving and taking went far beyond logic. No one should live as the Hindus did, bound by rules, ritual, arithmetic. The greatest possibilities lay beyond these.

"In the realm of the spirit," said Suren, "two and two don't make just four. They add up to so many intangibles besides. You and I aren't just two people. The fact that we're friends makes us more than two. There is so much else between us that we both draw on and gain from."

And the death of Christ, Suren had added, was a supreme example of this.

"How else can I believe that Christ died to save us?" he demanded. "How could one man's death save millions except in terms of the belief that whatever you love and serve becomes yours, and so it can affect and influence far beyond its time and its logical circumscribed limit?"

Far beyond its time, beyond even death. Though resurrection, Ram Krishan thought with a rare trace of bitterness, was the monopoly of Christ. Still, Suren had been right. Logic could be a lunatic. Viet Nam, after all, was the result of logic. To what end had such logic led?

16

Ram Krishan went straight to the pantry when he got back from office and poked around among the packets and jars on the shelves. There was a tin at the back with a few glucose biscuits in it. They did not look very appetising. He debated putting them out for tea. Or he could ring up the shop in the neighbourhood market and ask them to deliver a new tin of biscuits or some of the fresh pastries they received from a bakery every day. He remembered the days when servants had known how to make sandwiches and had warmed the pot before putting tea leaves into it. Those niceties belonged to a bygone age. So practically did servants. Ram Krishan did not miss either. He decided against ringing the store. Raj's lady friend with all the lakhs in her name would have to make do with just tea unless she wanted to risk a rather ancient biscuit.

Ram Krishan came out of the pantry pleased with his decision. He had a definite philosophy of housekeeping. It should take as little time and fuss as possible. Life was meant for doing the things one wanted to do, and for being in touch with the people one liked. He had never wanted a wife who laboured over a hot stove producing culinary triumphs, or one whose perfectionism gave her nervous breakdowns over the servants. He had made this clear to Vinita from the start. It had taken time for her to unlearn her ways, to undo the meticulous twentyfour-hour housekeeping that service of a husband involved, and that passed in their society for wifehood. And Ram Krishan had rejoiced at that gradual undoing. Their home, untidy and relaxed, had been welcoming. And Vinita as a result had never been much of a cook or a house-keeper. But what a friend and companion she had become! Some warmth from the past brushed him softly as he stood in the doorway to the living room watching the darkening sky. The grass so lately lime-coloured, looked grey in the draining evening light. He could hear Bindu moving about in the room behind him, sniffing mightily as he lighted the fire and rattled china. Bindu was a stop-gap as domestic help seemed to be nowadays. He wore an army sweater a size too large for him and dreamed of the army. He planned to join it the following year when he was old enough. Soon the fire was leaping cheerfully and the tea tray arrived to be set down on a table in front of it, miraculously timed for Raj's arrival.

A woman got out of the car in the shadows of the garden.

Ram Krishan had forgotten to replace the fused bulb at the entrance. He could not see her clearly but something in her attitude stirred a half-forgotten recollection. She stood there waiting, as though in a vacuum. He had seen people like her, sufferers of the Partition frenzy and havoc, on station platforms at Delhi. Their social status had for once made little difference. Whether they lay in tatters closely packed on the ground, their tin trunks and bundles wedged between human layers, or were better dressed and stood about, they were all quite oblivious of the deafening trundle of luggage barrows and the grinding and thundering of trains. The past had been dynamited behind them and there was no retreat. But the future was blank too. They were all going somewhere in search of it, waiting for trains—some that thundered by packed full, leaving them behind over and over again. Ram had been working with a refugee rehabilitation centre in those days and sometimes it had seemed to him that he, too, stood endlessly at the station in a nightmare in which trains came and went, wrenched and wailed and clanged. The whole world had been compounded of trains bordered and weighted with the density of human suffering, surrounded by a fog of dead hope. The horror of that world!

He remembered his duty as a host and came forward to greet his guests. In the shabby, comfortable, firelit living room his impression of Simrit altered a little. So this, Ram Krishan saw, was what withdrawal meant, this presence without affirmation or emphasis. It was the bare bones of living and the extras played no part in it. Is this what I am like? His sympathy for her was so acute that he passed a hand over his eyes to dispel it.

Raj, sensitive to Ram Krishan's moods, worried: I hope he has not switched off on us. He won't be much help if he has. And quite apart from that, there was the Ram Krishan, unique and rewarding to know, whom Raj loved and wanted Simrit to meet.

"Shall I pour the tea?" Raj asked.

Ram Krishan came to himself.

"What about Mrs Raman pouring it?"

Simrit smiled and moved to the chair near the tray.

There's extraordinary sweetness in that smile, observed Ram Krishan. And he began to wonder if what she had lost was replaceable. But was real loss ever replaceable? And could one go on from there, and if so, how? A queer agitation seized him, as if Simrit's problem and his own grew out of the same root and needed a common solution. He felt stirred by feelings long unused. As often when Raj was with him he thought of Raj's father, Suren, of words and sentences crystal clear across the years: "You can't make a virtue of renunciation, Ram," and his own quick disavowal of renunciation. What, after all, had he ever renounced or wanted to? But renunciation, he saw now, was also disuse. It was a sadhu with his arms held above his head until they could never be lowered again. It was eyes blindfolded until they lost their sight. It was living as he did, without striving. It was the desire to strive broken in two, laid on Vinita's pyre, burned with her and scattered with her ashes to the winds. And that must not happen to Simrit. He would not allow it to happen.

"Raj," he said, "this is a bigger room than my office. Smoke if you want to."

Raj acknowledged the concession with relief and exchanged a wink with Simrit.

"He's been telling you I am a cantankerous old man," said Ram Krishan. "Well maybe I am. I don't approve of his dirty smoking habit either. But not because of the cancer scare. In fact I'm not sure the West is on the right track there. I'm of the opinion that the mind and body are closely related in disease. It is something modern medicine in the West is having to face more and more."

Raj relaxed. Whatever had started him off on this tack Ram Krishan was going to be all right, forthcoming, perhaps even at his best, ripe and full of discussion. It was always a healthy sign when he began this way, about a subject not connected with the matter in hand. He was best when he was expansive.

"The West, you know," went on Ram Krishan, "has a way of waking up to a discovery all of a sudden, as if it were really something new under the sun. Take non-violence. Suddenly, but almost overnight, they see like a flash that violence is an evil. Till now it counted as a virtue—the conqueror in history, the all-conquering male in fiction, the survival of the fittest in the marketplace, and so on. It was a must. Now that it dawns on them that it is not the answer, that in fact it's a miserable failure, they are overcome by the discovery. It invades every pore of their activity. It's beginning to show in their policies It has already burst into their theatre, their songs, everything. We, on the other hand, have always recognized non-violence as a value but we've never given it form or shape, never popularized or institutionalized it, never even put it to music! No catchy songs about it that would capture the young, become part of the air we breathe. I don't count non-violence under Gandhi. There we followed the man, not the idea. The idea has remained vague and sentimental. That's why it hasn't really made an impact with us."

Ram Krishan took the tea Simrit handed him and sat back. He liked conversation to be pointed, not about polite nothings. He felt he had made a good beginning and wondered if they would take it up. Stirring his tea he realized that in this house no woman had ever poured tea for him.

Simrit said, "Yes, I have wondered about that often. I have wished non-violence had become a way of thinking, made into a law, or given some kind of sanction, so that it could be passed on like an inheritance. I've wanted to pass it on to my son. Until one can, it's no use."

"How old is your son?"

"Sixteen."

"It is already too late then. At this age he will not begin to value anything new. The gods he knows are the ones he will cling to."

"I am aware of that," she said.

She lifted sombre eyes to him. He could see the withdrawal again, almost visible in her face.

"So that's why," she said unexpectedly, "I have nothing to give my children, because I have nothing to give them except non-violence. That's an odd thing to say at tea-time, but you began it."

Her laugh had a tremble to it. She went on talking nervously.

"I mean, how do you give them non-violence in an attractive package, something they can be sure will work in the world around them, unless they see it working first?"

My dear, Ram Krishan wanted to say, my dear, don't be despairing. There is a world like that very near us, around the corner if you look for the signs. You in your lifetime may reach out and touch it, if you have the courage and the endurance, if you believe. He felt inexplicably moved. What, he wondered, was happening to him this teatime? The room seemed transfused with a quiet glow. What was more, it was a glow of the present, not of something remembered. It came from the three of them at that moment as they sat there. No voice from the past spoke to him at this juncture of peace. He had a sense of lightness and liberation, as if lifted out of long bondage. The present, he told himself, is holy ground for it is the past and the future in one. I stand on it. It matters. It contains all that there is. I must make more of it.

He said gently to Simrit, "It will work because people like you will make it work. My good friend, Raj's father, would have said: because Christ died for it. I would rather say: because we live for it."

The words encircled the three of them in affection and Simrit, relaxing in her chair said after a while without bitterness, without a headache starting at the thought of it: "What is so killing about this tax settlement is the thought that one person could deliberately do this to another. That's the kind of violence, the everyday kind, we must do away with first of all."

Ram Krishan fumbled in his pocket for his glasses.

"Now tell me about it, and let me see the agreement. I have only glanced through it."

Raj put the document on the table between them and explained its terms concisely. Ram Krishan listened and was profoundly shocked, for this was not a question of generosity or its lack. It was a denial of plain justice, the justice one dispensed even to a stranger, even to the enemy when war was over. He was astounded by the personality of the man who could dictate such terms and the complexity of motives that could carry a battle so far into the future, far beyond the end of the relationship. Even the most ruthless left a way of escape to the enemy. It was part of the unspoken creed even of war not to bomb what need not be bombed, nor to go on bombing after the target had been hit. There should be no needless destruction even in war—unless as sometimes happened, war made men go haywire and sanity no longer commanded their actions. Could that be the case here? He found himself deeply interested in the character of Som. The Consent Terms he could see were tilted finally and fully against Simrit, yoking her till the day she died to a load of tax that would cripple her capacity to earn. He listened to Raj's calculations. Simrit would, with those shares in her name, pay seventy-two per cent tax on her own earnings, quite apart from deposits like Annuity, and total surrenders like Wealth Tax. So there could be no question of her accepting these terms. They would have to be fought.

Ram Krishan, looking fuzzily at the room through his glasses, thought of his country beginning to look distorted like this room. Great ideals were in decay, with nothing yet, or for a long while to come, to replace them. Instead there was a mindlessness in which anything could happen. Ruthlessness could begin to look quite ordinary, and ordinary things appeared impossible. Nevertheless, he thought, we have to grasp the ordinary sane possibility by the tail if need be, grab it and force it to happen, at least insist on behaving as if it would. Or we shall all go beserk. One thing was certain. No enormity of this or any other kind could be voluntarily accepted. This tax settlement could not be hung on a woman unless one accepted barbarism as a daily event. No man he knew would have accepted it. He sat silent for a long time thinking of solutions and discarding them. A document like this would not, he was convinced, stand up in any court of law. But courts took years and cost money. And appeals followed court cases. The whole rigmarole would be wearily long and defeating, even if Simrit could afford it, and meantime she would still be hung with the horror of the settlement. There must be a straightforward release open to them. Anything as wholly unjust as this, it must be possible wholly and cleanly to reject. It should drop off of its own corruption.

"I think you must do the simple thing," he said speaking to Raj with authority, as it was Raj who had taken the problem on. "You must explain to the tax department exactly as you explained it to me, attaching the Consent Terms. Explain that since Simrit does not benefit from the shares they should be already regarded as a trust, which in fact they are, and pay their own taxes." He added with a faint smile, "That should be a new assignment for a free lance writer."

"What chance is there that the tax department will accept the explanation?" asked Simrit.

Ram Krishan was wondering himself. But the thing had to be caught by the tail, caught and nailed down and exposed for what it was, a naked brand of exploitation, all the more shameless because it was taken for granted.

"There is always a chance," he said out loud, "and however slim the chance, it has to be taken."

"Mind you," he added, "this is my opinion, not a tax expert's."

"The tax expert," put in Raj, "said there was hardly a chance in a thousand that any explanation would be accepted."

"Did he?" Ram Krishan was interested. "Well that settles it then. We must definitely go ahead with it."

Challenging the experts was something that stirred him to the marrow. He had done it all his life. Besides he had a mulish belief in the ordinary human being's sense of decency and justice.

"Of course," said Raj, "the man I consulted was not very interested in the case. He's in with all the big companies, earns huge fees, and Simrit is small fry."

Clear, cleansing anger went through Ram Krishan, leaving

him calm and certain. He would see this thing through.

"I have a suggestion to make," he said to Simrit. "Until it is settled, live as if you did not have this horror hanging over your head."

Once though Indians had been slaves, they had lived as if they had been free, heads held up, chests thrust out, invincible under Gandhi. And what price miracle if it had left not even a spark, if it could never happen again?

Simrit looked up, momentarily released from her anxiety by a sudden expanded awareness. The days ahead could be entirely hers. They were hers. There they were, like the blank sheet of paper she had looked forward to filling every morning. She could do as she liked with them, and whatever she did from now on would be her own personal achievement—or failure. She had known it before, but only in self-pity, never as adventure.

"Well, young lady?" The gaiety in Ram Krishan's eyes and voice was new and contagious, "That could be non-violence in action for you—the refusal to bend the knee, bow the head. What about it?"

"Yes," she said gladly, "that's what I'll do. At least I'll try."

She poured herself another cup of tea and was conscious of a deep positive pleasure in its strong fragrance, in the feel of warm china cupped in both her hands. With all his insistence on keeping her a woman Som had not realized how much a woman she was in her sensuous enjoyment of the moment. If Som had paused at all, some isolated unimportant moment might have held him, too. She was thinking of him quietly, distantly, without hurt.

"This tea is excellent," Raj said to her, "and you look happy." As if he understood that the two things were related.

"I am." she replied, and it was true.

She looked at Raj, deep in his chair, hands stuffed in his pockets, a posture of permanence and contentment unusual to him. So he can sit still, she noted.

"That carpenter didn't take his money, Raj," she said.

Her books stood in tall shelves tailored to their requirements by the gnome carpenter Raj had brought. He had hauled them up the stairs with the aid of two assistants, placed them against the wall and disappeared.

"He'll be back for it one of these days," Raj assured her.

"But—how odd. Why didn't he take his money?"

"That's your commercial past speaking. It isn't at all odd. He knows where you live and he'll be back. He's concerned about his payment all right, but he's easy about it. It's an old rule with a good craftsman, too, that the customer has to be satisfied."

Simrit had not handled money, except kitchen money before. Som, or his office, had paid all the bills. Everything had been docketed and dealt with by someone else.

"Another first for you, Simrit—your very own first bill to pay."

Watching them tease like children, Ram Krishan saw it happening, the fatal combine of love and friendship. Another thing he had untaught Vinita his little, known, orthodox bride, had been what other people understood by love. His own conception of it was clear. Love may be electric, but as time passed one found that though electricity was useful at night, it was not needed by day. It was when one got the milder food of friendship combined with physical love that escape was difficult. In the end there was nothing in the world stronger than friendship. These two, he felt, would enjoy even the distance between them. He yawned and felt empty and peaceful. The last vestige of his yearning for the past dropped from him and he wondered why. Perhaps because something of his had been passed on and would live through these two—which was the reason, after all, why men wanted children. He sat back comfortably, trying to decide if they knew it had happened to them.

In the car Simrit said, "I'd like to know him better. What an unusual man. His goodness reaches out."

"Yes," said Raj. "He did that to me all through my student days and still does on occasion, but the occasions have become rare. He more or less folded up after his wife died. But today I saw him at his best after a long time, the sort of teacher-pupil thing he's so good at, understanding and wanting to be understood. I really loved him as a boy. I learned a lot about friendship, knowing him. His was what a life should be, spread around and touching everything in its path with some of itself. Like the Bible says: 'Good tidings of great joy'."

"You quote the Bible a lot for someone who doesn't believe in it."

"It's queer that I have these doubts," he said, "because Christianity was a legend in my home. It was all around me, a living blazing thing. It had to be, with a father who had rebelled against his own father for its sake. But it wasn't enough for me as I grew up. I wanted to believe in it utterly but I couldn't. At college I felt closer to Ram Krishan on most issues than to my father. Ram Krishan seemed to have the bigger view, the more generous understanding—though I respected them equally as men. So you see I became a wanderer looking for a clue."

"Yes, I do see," said Simrit. She quoted softly from the Rig Veda, "O Faith, give us faith."

"Of course we're all looking for clues and I suppose some matters go to the grave with one unsolved. Ram Krishan goes on debating certain points raised by my father. They had a sort of life-long debate that should have ended with my father's death. But Ram Krishan goes on and on trying to straighten it out in his own mind."

"He understands how to straighten other people out," said Simrit. "I feel so refreshed. Remember him saying I should live 'as if' the Corpus wasn't hanging over my head?"

"When are you going to?"

"Stop the car, Raj."

He drew up to the side of the road and turned off the engine. Simrit took his face in her hands and kissed him lingeringly on the mouth. The gesture was gentle and maternal. It seemed to come from the soft unhurried depths of a relationship. It met a hankering in him for reassurance that the bond between them was reliable. The next moment he was entangled in a ritual that left no room for any hankering, and humbled by feelings he had never known.

"I think I fell in love with you," she said on the way home, "the day of the debate in Parliament."

"On oil!" said Raj. "I might have known love would dawn on you in the chilly chamber of the House in the middle of a debate about oil."

17

The day had been packed with activity, bringing a week's negotiations to an end. Sumer Singh felt an enormous pleasure that it was satisfactorily over. The Soviet Government was to undertake the geological survey of a large area north of the belt where oil had been discovered. And possibly, if it yielded its promise, pipelines, and later even a road, might link it up with oil-bearing areas in Soviet Asia. The prospect was thrilling for more reasons than oil. An oil empire connected by thousands of miles of road would be a vital factor in the politics of the region, and fantastically important for India. Control at home would have to be in the right hands, with men every inch committed to the new policy. *Now we're moving*, he thought with a shiver of excitement.

The morning meeting had been followed by a lunch at the Ashoka Hotel where there had been congenial conversation through interpreters and a lot of full-throated laughter. Sumer Singh had talked of India's resources and needs and the Government's desire for closer collaboration with the Soviet Union. His guests had drunk to the survey in orange juice and toasted their other joint ventures in steel, coal and pharmaceuticals. At the head of the table under the great chandelier, Sumer Singh knew that today at long last, he had come out from under the shadow of the old Minister. This was his own deal and the credit was his entirely.

They were, he had thought looking down the table, a remarkably attractive people, and part of their attraction lay in the single-minded creed — the consuming fire — that had moulded a backward peasant people into a massive world force. It was time it happened here — time to throw away sentiment, the weak, worn-out liberalism of the past, time to bury Gandhi and write a new page of Indian history. The winds of Asia had changed. The old connections belonged in the garbage can. The entire sentimental framework of Parliament and Constitution would have to be scrapped. Ultimately there would be a clean sweep — and today marked its beginning. For him, he was convinced, it meant big things ahead—the prize—the Foreign Ministership which in the coming reshuffle would almost certainly be his. He was sick to death of oil and its complications, the never-ending controversies about crude, about refinery agreements, and all the homework it meant. He did not want that Ministry. The Foreign Minister was a key figure on the world stage, or would be once the Eastern alliance took shape.

Tonight Sumer Singh needed to relax. The memory of Pixie sent a wave of warmth to his stomach. He recalled the first time he had met her and her awe at finding herself at such a "posh" cocktail party near the man whose picture appeared so often in the papers, the startled withdrawal of her hand when he had taken it. But once he had persuaded her of his interest she had given in. Later she had been openly admiring. "I read your speech in the papers today." Just those few words could transform her. It was not flattery, he could tell by one look at her face. It had all the eloquence her language lacked. She meant it. In an atmosphere where flattery abounded, Pixie was like a breeze from the mountains, a bracing tonic. He had never seen that look on any face nor ever been such a hero to anyone.

He telephoned just as Pixie was getting ready to leave the shop to tell her they would meet for dinner at the usual place at eight o'clock sharp, and she had promptly accepted as he had known she would. It was a quarter to nine when Sumer Singh let himself in and greeted her with a breezy impersonality. He poured himself a drink from a bottle he kept in the cupboard and looked over enquiringly at her.

"Haven't you got one yet?"

"I don't want one, thank you," said Pixie.

"Oh come on, don't be a little prig. I want to relax tonight and I don't like drinking alone."

"All right."

She took the glass he handed her and obediently held it.

"Drink up, you'll feel better," urged Sumer Singh.

He noticed how washed out she was looking, and sitting very stiff and straight in that upright chair gave her a severity that made her look much older. He missed her cheerfulness and compliance, the small services she usually performed for his comfort. She must be upset because he had broken his lunch engagement with her the other day and he was prepared to humour her a bit. But this was his evening and he was not going to let her spoil it. He got up and ruffled her hair. She continued to sit frozen.

"I — I wanted to talk to you," she said.

"Yes? What about?"

Sumer Singh stretched himself comfortably in the chair opposite, becoming more lazily aware of her presence, watching her cross and uncross her ankles nervously. The little waif was not herself today.

"I hope you realize," he bantered, "that you are in the presence of a man who has piloted a magnificent deal. This is a very special occasion."

He waited for the flicker of admiration that any reference to his work aroused in her. But Pixie was looking dull and frightened.

"What is the deal?"

"I shall tell you about it in a minute when you've settled down. Sit in that chair. It's more comfortable. You look all on tenterhooks."

She blundered, "I won't be able to come here any more."

"Nonsense. We can't meet anywhere else. It wouldn't be safe."

"I meant I won't be able to come at all."

"Don't be a damned fool, Pixie," he said heavily. "What are you afraid of? Has anyone seen you coming and going?"

"No. At least I don't think so. It's not that. I — don't want to go on with this."

"Do you realize," he said casually, "I gave you a place to live in and a job? Do you think either of those is easy to get in this city?"

Or anywhere else for her with no training, no qualifications, no influence, no college degree. She knew damned well that even with degrees, with training and confidence, there were lakhs without jobs. She was nothing and nobody compared with most of them. Pixie raised her eyes to his with an effort.

"I'm grateful to you. I really am. You've been very kind to me."

"Yes," he said thoughtfully, "I have. I don't think you have the least idea where you might have been today without the help I've given you. Of course there are jobs — for girls like you — "

"No!" she cried involuntarily.

"I would think it over then if I were you," said Sumer Singh.

Sumer Singh went to the bottle for another drink and held it up to her. She shook her head.

"There would be no hurry, of course, about your vacating your flat," he said, pouring whisky into his glass. "I'll see that you got a month's grace to find alternative accommodation. Of course with rents as they are — "

"And my job?" she asked hardly above a whisper.

"I daresay you can keep that—if the management is satisfied. I told you at the start there were no guarantees in the job."

"Would you put in a word?" she pleaded. "I mean so that I would have time to look for something else, in case they want to replace me?"

He dropped three cubes of ice one after another into his glass, holding them high with the silver tongs, making a game of it, and poured more Scotch over them. He took an appreciative sip and came back to his chair.

"This is the real stuff. The other day it was some awful bootlegging concoction. It left me with holes being drilled in my head. How did you feel next morning?"

"I? Oh I felt all right. I didn't take much and then I put such a lot of soda in it anyway — " her voice broke. She stopped abruptly and begged, "Please would you put in a word for me?"

"I suppose I could." He yawned widely. "Can't promise anything though. God, I'm tired. It's been a long day Pixie, and I have closed a superb deal. I'm going to have some dinner."

"What deal?" she asked dully. "Oh, I remember, you made a deal with the Soviet delegation."

Sumer Singh was helping himself to a plateful of food.

"I read about it in the newspaper," she said. "The newspaper I read said there was a Canadian offer, too, and you should have taken that."

He looked up amused.

"The newspapers are hardly in a position to advise what I should have done."

"Oh, I know," she agreed hastily.

"What else did the newspaper say?"

"It said something about keeping Russia and America out of that Jammu region. And it said this way a big piece of Indian territory will come under the Russians."

"Under their supervision naturally. It's oil exploration we're doing, not star gazing."

He was attacking his food.

"Yes, close supervision, the paper said," she remembered the phrase.

"Hang the paper," he said, "and go and get yourself some dinner. It's getting late. It's none of the papers' blasted business. They're an interfering lot. Which paper was this anyway?"

Pixie tried to remember and could not. But now her curiosity was roused.

"But why did you choose the Russian offer? I mean, I suppose it must have been the best one if you chose it — I was just wondering—" she tapered off.

"My dear Pixie, I appreciate your concern, but you should leave political matters to people cleverer than yourself. There are good reasons why I did what I did."

"I know there must be," she said anxiously. "I only wanted to know why — "

"Did you?" Sumer Singh put his plate away and helped himself to another drink.

He noticed she was not eating. Whether she stayed or went now did not much matter. She was the kind he could pick up twice a day if he cared to, anxious little strays, eager to please, grateful for his favours. But this one, he decided, would leave with no doubt about what she was losing. Food and drink settled in him, he felt a sense of power and a need to communicate it, to impress this nobody he would never see again. He began talking of the contract he had negotiated, the pages of printed material that would be a turning point for India and a personal triumph for him, putting him at the top of the Ministerial tree. If things went as he expected he would be a force to reckon with in his own party in a few months' time. Privately he knew he could already count on the support of both the Communist parties, too. And one or two of the other Leftist groups were solidly behind him. The vote on the oil offer had made that clear. And the Independents had not been much of a problem in the vote — thirty thousand rupees per vote was not too much to hand out when the stakes were global. Garg and some others had not been willing to bite but their elimination was now a matter of time. The irony of it was that it would all happen with such ease. The major change, when it came, would be voted in in the most faultless democratic manner. Upheaval would come later at the right time. It was important to observe the time schedule scrupulously.

"But how is it a good contract?" Pixie persisted, puzzled.

Sumer Singh mashed out his cigarette in the ashtray near him.

"Never mind. It's beyond you." Her ignorance seemed to put him in good humour. "The Russians are a great people and we have a lot to learn from them."

"Of course," said Pixie. "Like our people are great, too, in their own way," she said hesitantly.

Sumer Singh laughed but not with enjoyment.

"This people great?" He put down his glass. "They won't be great in a hundred years, unless we do something about it now to change them inside out, make a new people of them. A hundred years from now they'll still be whining and begging. I thought the labourers on my father's land were a whining begging lot, no better than their cattle, but the whole country's like that. We've got to get them into line, drill some purpose into them."

He accurately read the grief and bewilderment in her face, as though she were watching something precious burn. Many like her would react the same way. That was why there had to be a clean-up, a break away, an end to the Gandhi syndrome, that supposedly long, shining chain of service, begun by the Mahatma that he himself had spun out ad nauseam in speeches. He began to talk of the brand of revolution other countries had had, real revolution — not eyewash — and of all that ruthlessness alone could accomplish.

"Isn't there," she asked, painfully, "an Indian way for us to get ahead? Why must we get ahead the way other people have done?"

"What Indian way?" he said brusquely. "Don't be a fool."

"Anyway," said Sumer Singh, "that's enough about politics.

He patted his knee. "Come here."

Pixie stayed riveted to her chair.

"Well, what's the matter? It's a long time since we had a cuddle. And don't tell me you haven't anything to be grateful to me for."

She made an involuntary movement of recoil. Sumer Singh did not see it. He came over to her chair and pulled her up. Immediately Pixie tore herself loose in a fierce shuddering movement of revulsion that Sumer Singh understood at once.

"Get out," he ordered savagely, and as she did not move, "Get out before I throw you out. You're nothing but a cheap stray."

When she had gone he settled down with a fresh drink. An anaemic creature, Pixie, and her breasts were too meagre for his taste. All right for a little while but it was time for a change. The woman who came to mind was the lush, dark one he had seen at Shah's party. Shah would remember her name and arrange a meeting.

18

Ram Krishan looked through the morning paper without interest and put it down. He was very tired of politics. But Delhi and politics, all kinds, at all levels, were inseparable, and anyone who produced a weekly on national affairs had to live in Delhi. He could, of course, wind up the weekly. It did not make much money. But what would he do then? And live in Delhi he would no matter what. He had been born in the old city and watched the transformation of a great stretch of barren land into a new capital with official buildings and gardens of classical beauty. He had watched its new roads being marked, its trees being planted, seen it take shape in the hands of the thousands of masons, labourers and craftsmen who came from all over north India to transport stone, gravel and sand, hew rock, mix mortar, carry brick and cement, and engrave on stone and marble, skills their ancestors had learned from the Moghuls. He had even *heard* Delhi rise, woken up as citizens had been in those days by the roar of electrically propelled saws. Delhi might be a passing show for officialdom and for Parliamentarians. For Ram Krishan it was home.

He looked down at the tea tray his servant had brought. It was one of those good-looking, light metal affairs, easy to keep clean, only Bindu never managed to keep it so. He lifted the lid off the tea-pot. It was stained a patchy brown. So would the tea-pot be after Bindu emptied it of tea leaves and sloshed a little cold water round in it before putting it away. Ram Krishan who had no use for decor either as a status symbol or as a need of his own nature, cherished cleanliness. He had had to do without it since Vinita's death. Resignedly he poured his tea and tried once again to read his paper. He was hunting for a theme for his New Year issue and the paper gave him no clue.

It could be the time had come—or must be made to come—when politics would take a back seat. The new leadership would thrust up from other occupations and it would depend on what people in field and workshop and classroom and behind their managerial desks believed in. Indians needed no new political star to follow. They needed faith in themselves. For most of them it could still come through the way of life called religion. His New Year issue could be about this, taking the point of view that Hinduism must descend from its heights to become a source of strength and hope in the hut and the factory. Philosophy had no meaning unless it was a philosophy for the living. The corpse Jesus blest rose up and walked. That was the miracle Hinduism must perform today, touch and transform the lives of millions and give them a basis for action, not merely a scripture and a ritual. It had to, in a situation that had politically become impervious to reform. The reform had to come now from the heart of the crisis: the human being. He poured a second cup. It was hot and delicious.

Again and again he had come back to the problem in his own mind, and each time without an answer. It may be, he thought, that I don't find an answer and nor does Raj, because in India no single belief *has* the answer. Too many tides have crossed and blended here, produced mixtures in us that cannot now unmix. Why do I, for instance, think of Jesus and the corpse of Lazarus when I am thinking of Hinduism? Why should that simile spring to mind at all? Is it because of my education, because my generation and Raj's too, have had their feet in two worlds—and so each of us must contain both and draw on both or grievously waste part of ourselves? Whatever rigid choices have to be made elsewhere, ours is the ancient and seasoned soil of co-existence. It has held its contradictions tenderly, peacefully. This is where swords need never flash for the One Faith, religious or political. This is the land of Faith. And then Ram Krishan wondered if he did not sometimes get carried away by sentiment and by his years. It had all been true enough once but the future might hold something very different. And if that were so, there was no time to lose.

He began to think about how he would arrange the New Year issue, perhaps in dialogue form, with selected people giving their arguments. He would open the dialogue with the proposition that if the irreconcilables of Hindu and Christian belief could be sorted out, a powerful answer and a new basis for action might be found for India.

He called to Bindu to take away his tray and bring his breakfast in an hour and a half and started his walk around the block. It was an enchanting morning, bright and pure, as it was for so brief a time in winter. He came home, bathed, breakfasted and sat down to write. The moment seemed somehow propitious. The sun on his study floor warmed the whole room. It lay half across his desk like a benediction. The silence was serene. Bindu had given him his bazaar account for yesterday, taken the day's order and gone off on Ram Krishan's bicycle to the market half a mile away. He would not return for two hours after visiting friends and relations, and incidentally doing the marketing. The bicycle tube and tyres would soon need changing again. Bindu was a furious peddler.

The real conflict between Hinduism and Christianity, Ram Krishan wrote, was that Christianity believed in the superiority of value over existence. God must—first and foremost—be good. Hinduism was more concerned with the existing state of affairs. He began to elaborate the point: Christians take as their starting point the good they find in their daily experience and try to improve things around them. So religion for the Christian is a concern—a persistent concern—with the good. The Hindu, on the other hand, stresses existence and acceptance. There is no question of improving the existing state of affairs, only of gracefully adapting to it, to both the good and evil of the universe.

Ram Krishan stared out of the window. How to resolve a conflict like that, fundamental and final, dividing as it did two streams of humanity—one, vital, active, aspiring, the other in danger now of stagnating and thereby of giving way to some rough, alien, immediate attraction?

He put down his pencil and looked out of the window. Two tendencies seemed to develop in one side by side as one grew old, he reflected. One saw *through* events to the future, as if corridors led outward from them to what was going to take place. There was no doubting the veracity of that vision. It was broad, clear, *happening.* And along with this, one saw and heard things here and now with a complete clarity never before achieved. The sound of a blue-bottle buzzing drowsily against the window-pane was astonishingly distinct. The hibiscus on the hedge looked intensely scarlet. Is it only in me, he wondered, or does this happen to everyone? Do people who lead rather sedentary lives develop this capacity to receive startling messages of form and colour, or has it something to do with advancing age? Raj would not have it, he was sure, but Simrit might.

A cough at the door announced Bindu. Ram Krishan turned around irritated.

"I forgot to say the cooking oil is finished. I need more money."

It was no use telling Bindu the store would give him credit. Bindu enjoyed cycling. Ram Krishan took some money out of his wallet and handed it to the boy.

"Supposing I can't get cauliflower?" he asked.

"You will get cauliflower," said Ram Krishan. "The vegetable shops are piled high with cauliflower. Every garden is growing them too. It is the season."

"But if I can't get cauliflower, can I bring peas?"

"Very well," said Ram Krishan.

He knew better than to argue. Bindu preferred peas. He had serious doubts about an army career for Bindu, on which the boy's heart was set. He had a thorough-going enthusiasm for what he himself decided.

"And now I don't want to be disturbed till lunchtime," said Ram Krishan.

He turned back to his desk. The problem of religion,

he went on writing, is the problem of evil—poverty, disease, earthquakes. Some evil can be cured by human effort. Some cannot. How do Christian and Hindu tackle this problem? The Christian believes a good God could not have created evil, so evil is entirely separate from the good, unaccounted for and inexplicable. But for the Hindu, God is the universe itself. Man, he says, mistakenly regards certain things as evil because of his incomplete knowledge of the whole universe. Actually from the viewpoint of the whole, God's viewpoint, all things are good.

A bird sang its heart out in the creeper outside the window, and Ram Krishan looked up. He read the last paragraph he had written. Where does that get the Hindus, he worried. Maybe disease and poverty are illusions, but they still cause suffering. As far as I am concerned, my pain is my pain and there are no two ways about it. Illusions that have tremendous repercussions for the lives and outlooks of human beings cannot be lightly dismissed. In mortal eyes, evil is evil.

The telephone rang. Ram Krishan swore under his breath. He went out to the hall to answer it. He kept planning to have it placed in his study, or getting the wire extended so that it could be carried to whichever room he was in. But it was the kind of practical job he never got done. He spoke distantly into the receiver, his mind on the problem he was working out.

"Sorry," said Raj, "you were working."

"I was."

"I had to tell you I completed Simrit's tax returns and wrote a letter to the department about her situation. I want you to see the letter before I post it."

Ram Krishan recalled the Consent Terms. A hundred years from now, or in the limbo of eternity, Simrit's tax miseries would not matter. Today they did, illusory or not. He told Raj so.

"Yes, of course they matter. That's the whole point. That's why we're going to see this through." Raj sounded buoyant.

"I hope Simrit sees the point," said Ram Krishan. "The battle seems to be joined between you and the Consent Terms."

There was a brief pause. Raj said, "Yes, I know exactly what you mean. But there's a change."

"That's good news. That speaks well for my New Year number."

"For what?" asked Raj.

"Nothing. Bring your letter round to show me today."

Ram Krishan went back to his study. Now where was he? Stuck with the problem of evil, existent, inexplicable, incurable. How did religion face the fact? He made two columns on a clean sheet of paper.

The Christian says, he wrote in the first column, that there is evil, but there is more good. God is found in order, in reason, and in much of nature. The religious man wishes to increase the amount of good in the universe. Aspiration is a fundamental part of his philosophy. He is forward-looking, progressive. He has a desire for improvement, for reform, and great faith in human will and effort. He does not compromise with evil. He cannot consider it part of the good. His God may not be all-powerful, but he is all-good.

The Hindu, he wrote in the second column, has a very different approach. He accepts evil along with good. Evil is not his own personal pain or sorrow but the working out of a larger plan of which he is only a small and insignificant part. In any great system the parts count less than the whole and in a well-ordered universe the parts must be limit ed. This is not cowardly resignation. It is adaptation. No soaring aspiration, but in its place an overwhelming sense of the insignificance of the individual as compared with the universe. His attitude can be summed up: However much I suffer, my suffering is as nothing in the eyes of God.

Ram Krishan put down his pencil and read the two columns again. It seemed that nothing in the world could be resolved unless these two viewpoints could somewhere meet, each give the other its strength. What a fabulous inheritance, he marvelled, one nearly two thousand years old, the other immeasureably older, and, we still keep them apart, in different boxes, as if wisdom could be so apportioned and have the benefit it was meant to. It had to be joined—united in an ocean of strength if it was to combat the genius of Marx. If these two streams did not now unite, then their part in history might soon be over. Christian and Hindu would join the blood and waste in the gutters. He tried to overcome his sense of foreboding, but it was there, at the end of one of those corridors of thought, like an empty echoing building awaiting habitation.

The thing, then, was to find the common philosophic ground between them. The meaning of any religion was devotion to the good. People like myself and Simrit and so many others, Ram Krishan pondered, are deeply religious. That awareness of good, of God, of the universe, whatever one called it, was pervasive and supreme. It descended to the dust of the village. It was everywhere. It had to be made to yield results, to become a song on one's lips, a great fighting strength—and it was not, today.

Why not, why not, he wondered, and the answer he knew was a hair's breadth away. He wrote rapidly. We are, after all, considering the meaning of religion for people in their daily lives, from their own finite viewpoint. And according to that evil is definitely evil, whatever it might ultimately be. So there is no real conflict between the Hindu and the Christian. The Christian works for greater good in the universe, the Hindu for a more complete view of the universe. For both God is the source of value and he is all good. The difference between them is there but it is not final.

Ram Krishan's room was in shadow. The sun had shifted to another part of the house. He felt a little stiff and got up to stretch his legs. He went onto the verandah, hardly more than fifty feet square, and stood looking out. There was Bindu returning. The sights and sounds of late morning greeted him, the bus that trundled past his gate at this time every day, the woman next door who came out of her house to gather up her washing and peer into two glass jars filled with pickled vegetable. I like it better here, Ram thought, than in any other verandah anywhere else. This is my particular fifty square feet. These sights and sounds are home to me. And that's how it is with my philosophy. The vision a man works with has to be familiar enough to be understood. It's through that, firmly held, that he embraces the earth. It took more than courage to break with the past as Suren had done. It took revelation. And that came to few. For himself, for Simrit, for most people there were no acceptable breaks, no revelations. There was only abiding time, stretching back into antiquity, forward into the future. And that historic span contained the Christian view, and went beyond it. Good and evil may be separate channels as Suren the Christian believed, but so were parallel lines. Yet they met in infinity. Infinity, Suren, Ram Krishan said to his long dead friend, is the state where differences merge. Infinity is beyond good and evil. When you understand that the differences between us are resolved.

Ram Krishan had a profound sense of peace, feeling at last he had cleared an old misunderstanding. He was as sure now of his answer, tranquil and inviolable, as he was of the messages of colour and form his brain received. The answer was no mystic's vision but a picture seen in perspective. It had always been there, but now it was like a city emerged from a misty shroud, the lines of its buildings clean, hard and geometrical, its pillars and arches in classical juxtaposition.

He went outside, ready for his lunch, remembering with satisfaction that Simrit's tax letter was going to be posted today.

19

Simrit had been working all morning. Near lunch time when she got up from her desk, she was still wound up in the taut mechanism of writing. In the kitchen her hands were deft, cutting vegetables with precision. Not a slip of the knife or an unnecessary movement. Desk discipline lay over her, insulating her, controlling her actions. But her thoughts moved light and free.

The desk spell began to wear off. She put down her knife and the time of day flowed silkily into her receptive senses. She reached high for the ceiling, stretching her fingers, experiencing an exquisite slow release. Suddenly she felt reck-ess. She wanted to exaggerate, overflow, tell the world about the wild, sweet, heart-rending rapture of being alive.

"Mama, what are you doing?"

Brij and Jaya stood in the doorway. Simrit crossed her arms to embrace herself. If she had ever torn herself to bits for them, here she was given back whole in their youth and beauty. She felt unspeakably moved as she looked at them, unspeakably powerful and sheltering.

"Mama, you look so — different," puzzled her daughter.

"Do I sweetie? How?"

"Like a saint," said her daughter finally.

"A saint!"

"Here let me get that for you." Her son reached up easily to the top shelf for vinegar.

"Yes, you know how they look in pictures, quite ecstatic with lit up halos, even when they've got arrows going through them."

"I think they look stupid," said Brij.

"Oh don't be childish, Brij," said Jaya severely, and studying her mother's face critically she added, "Mama, you look full of juice."

"A juicy saint!" said Brij.

The children went into peals of laughter.

"You are the limit," scolded Jaya, recovering. "Why d'you have to go spoiling it? Can't you see she's looking different?"

"She isn't looking any different to me, and she's okay without being a saint. Too much saint talk and we won't get any lunch."

"You're just a lump," said Jaya, exasperated, "you don't know how to make conversation."

"What d'you mean I don't know how to make conversation? I've heard you making conversation and it's daft."

He pulled his sister's hair.

Simrit washed her hands at the sink and dried each finger lovingly.

She said, "Lunch is all ready. I was just making the salad. Now how would it be if I go out and leave the two of you to take care of the others?"

"No," they chorused.

"Well all right," agreed Jaya reluctantly.

"Wonderful," said Simrit, "because I think I'll go and have lunch with Raj."

"Where? At his place? We've never been to his place."

"We'll have a party at his place soon."

She kissed each of them. "I must run."

Simrit was half awake under blankets, timeless and peaceful, all of her a mingled, mellow whole. She was conscious of Raj in the tips of her fingers. Her skin and hair felt him. She lay absolutely still, unwilling to become part of segmented ordinary life again. Everything till now had been a preparation for Raj. Even her break with her past made sense, leaving her free to come to him today untouched at last by a shred of doubt.

She went over the past hour in her mind. She had arrived and rung his bell, her face cold and fresh from the wind, and he had opened the door with a look of either unbearable pleasure or pain, or a strange mixture of both, in his eyes. She was not even aware she had moved from the door but somehow they had come together swiftly and in panic, as if their own bodies stood in the way of this meeting. From the beginning they had been in step, lovers from another lifetime, forging an intimacy deeper than any she had ever known. Simrit went back to sleep.

When she woke, she felt carefree and festive, pitying all the people who could not laugh and talk and be light hearted when they made love. Raj must have been born with a natural understanding of this, seeing her as she had often seen herself—pulling love-making apart into all the bits of life it was, not a performance in which one had a role. Glittering, faintly familiar words hung suspended not far away, a glowing jewelled litany: "I nothing lack for I am His and He is mine forever." Nothing lack. They glittered there like an omen describing her fulfilment. She raised her head to see them better. The effort made her sit up and the plaque in the light from the half-open door of the next room revealed the lines above it: "The King of Love my Shepherd is whose goodness faileth never." There was a garland of pink roses she could now see, painted round the bright gold lettering. She repeated the words to herself. Good tidings of great dancing joy, invigorating, uplifting. She folded the blankets back, got up and began to dress. Life was very much worth living.

Raj relaxing in an armchair in the next room looked as if utter tranquility were a new sensation he were coping with for the first time, though his face was set and thinking. A man, she knew, who never forgot himself, except completely and by choice.

He made room for her on his chair.

"When I last looked in you were sound asleep."

"I woke up with the light from here shining on that wall plaque," said Simrit.

"It's a memento from childhood, practically the only one I have — rather crude-looking but I've always loved the hymn."

"I suddenly need to make a vow," she announced.

"Make it then."

"But what to? It has to be to something vast and impersonal, and yet to something close like this chair we're sitting on."

"That certainly makes it more complicated," said Raj, lazily adding, "and the Rig Veda and Aurobindo don't come up with any suggestions!"

"Nor does the Bible," she retorted.

"You're wrong there. The Bible would have hundreds if we got down to looking for some."

She stopped him from getting up.

"D'you know why I came? It was to tell you I'd got rid of my guilt. It was gone without a trace and in its place there was a strong, positive feeling. If feelings had smells, this one was a clean, carbolic, disinfectant smell —"

"There's a limit," protested Raj, "to being down-to-earth."

"So I just came to tell you about it. I never imagined—"

"All the rest?"

"And *that* was so unexpected too."

"More carbolic?"

"It was as if we hadn't."

Raj threw back his head and laughed.

"I doubt if any man would take that as a compliment."

"It's not a compliment, it's a —" she concentrated, searching for the right phrase, "fantastic piece of luck."

And with that Simrit threw away the barriers between the things that could be admitted and all those that could not, and described her fantastic luck as animatedly as she had the river and the cliffs on the journey to Kulu. When she had finished she slid out of the chair and looked around the room she had scarcely seen. It was plainly furnished except for one or two distinctive pieces obviously his own. The red carpet, she knew, must be his and the embroidered curtains and all the colourful pottery ashtrays. She took in the scene and her eyes came back to rest in his.

"That's all there is," said Raj, "nearly everything I have. I don't have a set-up either. No family, no frills. I've never missed any of it."

"I know."

"But you would. You nearly wept because you had to order a bookcase from scratch. You want a set-up and pedigree and everything in fine working order. Building from scratch is a misery and a bore."

"I could learn," said she.

"Is there anything to eat?" she demanded. "I'm starving."

In the kitchen Raj told her. "I had another talk with Shah's lawyer today about your problem. He says it's lucky your income doesn't come out of those shares because soon they aren't going to produce much income."

"Not produce an income—all those shares?"

"No. He says the way things are going shares will fall drastically and there may be a ceiling on dividends. Something like that. Maybe by the next session of Parliament."

"As soon as that?"

"If something even more drastic doesn't happen, like a seizure of shares. Of course if that happens," he said thoughtfully, "it will turn a lot else upside down too, and the Corpus will simply vanish into limbo."

"Fat old thing," said Simrit absently, frying eggs.

"Simrit, you really must show more respect for the Corpus. All those lakhs! At least until some other coinage comes into use. Like kindness."

"Loving kindness," murmured Simrit, taking his hand and rubbing her cheek against it. "Raj, is there ever going to be a time when we're not going to be talking about my silly tax problem?"

"There'll always be problems — and we'll have plenty of

time."

"What makes you so certain of whatever you say and do?" she asked enviously.

"A very unusual capacity known as thinking for oneself."

Simrit made a face at him.

"Anyone would think the rest of us were nitwits," she grumbled.

"What else can you call people whose lives are run by 'destiny'?"

He took the plates from her and carried them into the living room. For her sake he would have liked a ceremony of sorts—candlelight, flowers, flourish. To him the fried eggs and toast looked good and domestic on the clean white cloth and he felt he had known her all his life. Since meeting Simrit he had remembered more of his childhood than at any time before. "For what we are about to receive...." The grace of his father's house came back to him. He repeated it to himself now. But may be she would have preferred a little glamour, a bottle of wine, a touch of sophistication from her past. He looked at her in mute apology. Simrit came into his arms.

"Poor Moolchand," she said unexpectedly.

"Who on earth is Moolchand?"

"Som's lawyer, don't you remember?"

"Why poor him, and why now?"

She lifted her face to his.

"I feel sorry for everyone who isn't us, but specially for Moolchand. He's so *devoted* to the Corpus, and not only to it but to the whole idea of it. *Poor* Moolchand."

"Simrit," said Raj, "always look at me like this — even if you have to think of Moolchand every time."

20

There were already three people with Papa when he got there and then it started becoming a cocktail party—at twelve noon. Papa had asked Brij to the house to talk about his future before he left for Europe that afternoon and he was going to take him out to lunch. But Brij found Moolchand and two other men from the Company there when he arrived, and soon the door bell was ringing and more and more people arriving. He wandered into the bedroom. Papa's maroon plaid suitcase stood ready and the smaller matching one was lying open on the bed, with the bearer putting shaving things into it. And beside it was his briefcase. A smell of tobacco clung around. Brij sniffed deeply. The bearer was saying the whole place was going to be painted in Sahib's absence. But it hardly needed it, thought Brij He went back into the drawing room.

"Oh there he is. Does he know how to make a gin and lime?"

The speaker, thought Brij, was extremely stupid looking Too many rings and bangles, thick blocky heels on her shoes showing below the edge of her sari, heaven knows what all on her eyes, and a voice like a baby's. As he looked around the room seemed to fill with women like her and men, laughing hilariously and sitting on the arms of each other's chairs. He did not remember seeing a single one of these people at the house when Mama used to be here, except the Company people and he couldn't decide whether this was their natural behaviour or put on for the party.

"He's a sportsman," he heard his father say, "not used to waiting on ladies. Brij, get some beer out of the frig."

Papa's face was flushed. It got that way from drinking and laughing.

There were rows of beer and rows of Cokes lined up in the frig. Ordinarily he could have had three Cokes at one go, but he didn't feel like it. He was very hungry. When on earth were he and Pa going to have lunch and to talk? He went back with the beer. The stupid looking one was drinking gin and lime somebody else had mixed. Brij knew exactly how to mix one. For the last long-term break he had gone home with Rishad and they had experimented with several sorts of drinks. They had felt rotten afterwards but you had to try these things sometime.

"Mm. Isn't he goodlooking! Takes after Daddy," the baby voice said.

Oh shut up, thought Brij. He tried signalling a message

to his father but Pa seemed to be having the time of his life and his words were starting to slur. Pa could drink most people under the table and drive a car afterwards but he never could stop his words slurring. So people thought he was drunk when he wasn't and they never realized when he actually was. Brij idled in the hall, picking up an old magazine from the table, but now they had put records on the player and what with the music bouncing, and the party noise, he couldn't even read. He put the magazine away. He loved parties. Any other day he would have had fun, put the records on himself, even mixed a drink for Stupid. But today every minute disappearing into noise was an agony of waste. There was so little time left for his father to leave, and by the time he came back from Europe Brij would be back in school, and Pa never visited the school at all. So when would they decide about his future? Not till next summer, an eternity away. He had hoped he could tell Rishad about it as soon as school opened. He had wanted to go back knowing, the safe happy feeling inside him. His tummy was rumbling and he ate some popcorn. But the emptiness seemed to be spreading right through him.

"Brij, will you bring some more beer?"

He took more beer into the drawing room and now his father's eyes had that look they had when he'd been drinking. And that meant there'd be no talking, because Pa was really in the party now. He was making a date to meet one of these jokers in London next week, jotting it down in his diary. Well if they were meeting next week in London what on earth was the point of meeting them here today and wasting all this time with them? At two o'clock Brij was ravenous and decided to eat what he could find in the frig. There were tomatoes, butter and a tin of cheese. He was taking them out when the bell rang, and he went to answer it. It was Mrs Farrow with his father's ticket. Her smile vanished when she saw him standing there.

"What are you doing with those tomatoes all by yourself?" she asked. He looked down at them feeling foolish.

"Wasn't your Pa taking you to lunch today? What's all that racket going on in the drawing room? And it's past two. Time for him to be leaving soon."

Brij stood dumb.

Mrs Farrow took the tomatoes from him, looking sterner than he had ever seen her, and she muttered away under her breath as she walked ahead of him into the kitchen.

"I'll give Pa his ticket," Brij found his voice.

"You never mind the ticket," she said gruffly. "You stay right by me."

The bearer was there but she sat down on the kitchen stool and made him a thick sandwich, piling slices of tomato on cheese which he ate standing up. Mrs Farrow kept grumbling all the time. Criminal the way they only thought of themselves, these rich. Thought if they handed the little fellow a fat allowance and left him a fortune when they died, they'd done their duty.

"That's better," she said when he had finished.

Brij had a longing to fling himself onto her big warm lap and hide his face in her bosom.

"When are you and I going to the pictures, my lad?"

"Let's go soon," he brightened.

She nodded. "All right. I have to go now. Will you take this ticket in to your Pa."

Brij saw her to the door and went back to the kitchen. He found half a bottle of milk in the frig and drank it. All his health and strength booklets emphasized the food drill, the protein requirements, milk and meat especially, and he didn't want to lose an ounce or fall below the prescribed standard for a second. He had a horror of frailty in any form, and there was so much of it around, the emaciated thinness, the spindly-legged, narrow-chested look of people who never had enough to eat. He felt decidedly better after he had drunk the milk. The music had stopped. People were starting to leave. Some had already gone, and Papa had disappeared from the drawing room. Brij found him changing into one of his going-abroad suits.

"I didn't know it was so late," he said, "and I was going to give you lunch."

"That's okay, I just had a sandwich," said Brij.

"You did, did you?" said Pa. "And who said a sandwich is enough for a tough fellow like you. A sandwich is chicken feed. And a promise is a promise."

He took thirty rupees out of his wallet.

"Get something special to eat on the way home."

"Oh no Pa. Don't bother about that."

Pa caught him in a bone-crushing hug, lifting him clear off the floor. They were both laughing and breathless.

"Don't argue with me just because you've got all that muscle. I can still lift you right up."

"Can I come with you to the airport?"

Pa was knotting his tie in front of the mirror.

"Yes. How do I look?"

"Terrific," said Brij. "Is that from Cardin, too?"

"It is. You have a very well-dressed father."

Brij grinned in agreement.

Pa called to the bearer to go to the restaurant at the corner and bring him meat and *rotis* to eat.

"But what about all those people still in there," said Brij.

"They can stew in their own juice—or in my Scotch—it's amazing what a lot of friends one has when there's booze around. I'm going to eat in here. It's too late to go out now."

The food arrived and Brij watched him eat it with a relish that only Indian food had for his father when he'd been drinking. It had been like that in the old days too—Pa getting the servants' *rotis* to eat when he came back from a cocktail party. Now he was eating heavily, concentratedly, almost like a man in prayer, chewing every mouthful with deliberation, savouring every morsel, as if the whole world were shut out. It was so strange, Pa sitting here in his own room, away by choice from the others, about to leave for Europe, so terrifically dressed, always in the latest, the best, but eating bazaar food like that, the only food he ate like that, as if it filled some enormous chasm in him with much more than food. Pa—the queer tightness began in Brij. It must not start now, that futile agony to undo in imagination what the grown-ups had done. He swallowed hard.

"Pa?"

"What, son?"

"About my future, you were going to—"

"It's all decided. All settled. You're going abroad when you leave school, exactly a year from now."

"*What?*" Brij could hardly believe it. No ifs, no maybe? Papa looked up.

"That's what you wanted, isn't it?"

"Oh Pa!" Brij flung himself at his father.

"Hey!" Pa laughed, putting his empty plate aside. "You don't want the Managing Director boarding the plane with grease on his shirt, do you?"

He got some of the old "If" tone back in his voice.

"Mind you, this doesn't mean you can slack off and do as you please. You've got to work hard and get a first just the same. Schools abroad are very particular about past records."

"Of course!" Brij breathed. 'Oh Pa."

The dread didn't attach to the "If" any more. His doubts had lifted and he knew where he was.

"We'll work out the details later," said Pa. He added, "Oh, and I'd like you to move in with me when I get back."

"Here?"

"Yes, naturally."

Brij's head reeled with it. A room of his own, the record player with all the tapes and he could learn to drive—and go around in that car—

"I must get going," said Pa

For heaven's sake, some of them were still there in the drawing room, including Stupid, but Brij didn't mind them any more. Pa went over and patted Stupid's head, pinched her cheek and bent to say something in her ear that sent her into small shrieks. For heaven's sake, he'd only patted her head like he'd do with any dog. They went out, followed by all the stragglers. Then he and Papa got into the car, shutting the others out, and they were on their way to the airport in the cold brilliant afternoon. Pa turned toward him and his look, warm, possessive, electric—the only look in the world—went right into Brij. I'll never never let him down, pledged Brij, never as long as I live. And then he gave himself up to the road, the speed, the flying shining progress of the car.

21

The room took on a yearning in her imagination. She
and Som had shared it for six years, as long as they had
lived in that house. Reminders of it came thrusting through
memory, starting with the gay handloomed bedspreads.
There was a big round glass-topped table in the centre of
the room with two easy chairs flanking it, and a flamboyant
oil painting she had chosen hung above the beds. She was
certain she shouldn't go back. The question had not arisen
until Som's phone call the very day the phone was installed.

"Simrit?"

"Yes?" Her own voice had sounded strained pretending

not to recognize his, and then she felt compelled to say "Som?"

"Yes, how are you?"

"Very well," she replied.

"I've been away."

The longed-for friendliness was there. She could even detect an undertone of warmth. Earlier it would have bound her wounds. It was capable of that. It had always been a voice to rouse emotion, promising more than its owner was willing—or perhaps had the power—to give. Not calculatedly promising, but because it was that kind of voice.

"Are you there, Simrit?"

"Yes. Brij told me about your trip. I didn't know you were back already. He wanted to meet you at the airport."

"I came back earlier than I expected. There wasn't time to let him know. Now—" with that single word the tone changed imperceptibly, "Moolchand gave me your message about the Consent Terms. You didn't say there was anything wrong when you signed them."

Forgotten tension returned and fluttered in the pit of her stomach. One phone call did that. She mustn't go back to the room.

"I didn't understand the terms properly until afterwards."

"Well, we can meet and talk about it."

The tension in her gave a frightening leap.

"Would you like to come here? We can't very well talk comfortably in a public place," he said.

That was when the room had taken over in her imagination. She had kept flowers pressed under the glass top of the table. And there were studio pictures of the children angelically posed, across an angle in one wall, in identical curly silver gilt frames. She had left those there, pitying Som.

"Will that suit you?"

"Yes," said Simrit.

They agreed to a time and she arrived to be ushered into the bedroom by a new servant. She wondered how she had known beyond doubt that they would meet in this room whose every object was familiar to her. It had really been her room where she had spent hours at a time, and his only at night. It was, she could see, still hers, nothing altered, though the drawing room she had walked through was refurnished and still smelled of new paint. She realized he no longer used this room at all. It looked preserved, an exhibit in a museum for visitors to look at through glass. A small fresh pain started in her, not a longing for the past, but a kind of historic nostalgia. In a curious way nothing had either changed or ended. We've ended it, but it's going on with an uncanny persistence of its own. The most tenacious things were the intangibles, above all plain ordinary life lived over the years. In some inescapable way a part of her would always be married to Som.

They sat in the easy chairs and she noticed the pressed flowers where she had left them, violets from a springtime in Kashmir, sweet peas from their garden. Som began talking about her, reasonably and naturally, asking about the flat, her new life. Her fright lay lulled. She lifted her guards. She was in her own room. And they had, after all, shared a marriage.

Then he asked, "Well, what's the problem?"

Something had changed. Simrit could not remember herself and Som ever sitting down to discuss a problem. She told him about it though it seemed foolish to be telling him the facts and figures he already knew of a document he himself had dictated. But now at least he knew she understood the terms and would not accept them.

"I've had a talk with Moolchand," said Som. "What we can do is make a new agreement. Let's say you can use the income from those shares—if you don't marry—and until they're transferred to the children. Of course I'd have to stop the support you're getting now. And you'd have to pay the taxes on the Corpus, but since you'd be using the income that would be quite fair."

Simrit focussed on the violets, horrified at the bland ferocity of his proposal.

"But you'd still control the shares," she pointed out.

"Well of course. Buying and selling shares isn't much in your line, is it?"

"And I couldn't transfer them to the children earlier to save myself from the tax burden."

"The Corpus," said Som, "cannot on any account be touched or transferred by you. You don't understand. I want this money kept intact for Brij till he's old enough to handle it."

And what would happen to support for the children if she married, and how would she make ends meet for years and years before they finally were twenty-five years old, every one of them? Som had summoned her here not for a reprieve but another form of execution. Shah's lawyer's warning about the shares echoed in her ears: to depend on a share income in these changing political times would be treacherous. The lawyer could be wrong, but should she take a risk so great? Primed with the facts and dangers she felt she was standing on the edge of a precipice, an inch away from certain death, while Som smilingly invited her to jump. It took her breath away.

She could hardly believe it—after all these years to find that Som was a man without pity or concern, or even real responsibility. A man, she decided, not quite out of the jungle. He's so like Sumer Singh, she concluded in surprise. They're two of a kind though they might be on opposite sides of the fence politically—big business and radical politician. There's no *human* difference between them. Raj had said the real dividing line in Indian politics would soon be between the ruthless and the compassionate. All the other labels and variations would not count. And now she knew what he meant.

"Well, will that do?" Some asked. "It's a generous offer. I'm afraid I can't do better than that."

He really believed she would accept the new terms. It was such an outlandish idea, she could not even quarrel with it.

"But Som, don't you see I'd be in an even worse mess than I am now, even more at your mercy than under the present arrangement?"

He frowned, "You always had a penchant for the dramatic. At my 'mercy'! The words you use!"

"Besides," continued Simrit, "you know how unpredictable economic policy is—"

"My dear Simrit, I can't be held responsible for government's economic policies."

No, but you'd be dead sure that what you lived on was safe should anything happen, she said to herself. The room took on more of a museum cast than ever, sealed, preserved, easy to abandon, as something could be that was not firmly part of one's life. What about the new paint, the new furniture, the rest of the house? But those could be abandoned, too, as new things all along the road to betterment had been. This whole solid-seeming household could be masking a planned preparation for flight. Som would simply get up and leave, and live on the fat of some other land. Was that going to be the end to his adventuring? In her mind's eye she saw the Indian future as Shah's lawyer described it, unpredictable, and she knew with stubborn resolution that she would never leave India for any reason under the sun.

Som was getting restless.

"Well, will that do?" he said again.

Simrit got up to go. "No it won't."

"Then the present arrangement will have to do. The whole point, I wish you'd understand, is to safeguard the Corpus."

"Oh I understand that all right," said Simrit. "What I can't understand is what it's being safeguarded *for?*" She picked up her handbag and said, "Suppose stocks and shares just disappeared—as I'm told they might—what d'you suppose the children and I would live on?"

He shrugged, "My dear girl, you can't expect me to provide for every possibility."

She moved toward the door.

"Wait a minute. I'm planning to send Brij abroad next winter when he finishes school."

"He gave me the news," said Simrit.

"I'll have to take him over, of course, I want him to move over to me as soon as possible. I'd say immediately. I spoke to him about it before I left and he agreed."

A weight seemed to press down on her, making it hard to speak. Brij had not told her that part of it.

"I'll send the car for him. Can he be ready in an hour?"

"He'll be lonely," said Simrit quietly.

"I don't think so. He may miss Jaya but he's outgrown the other girls."

"I meant he'll be lonely without something—a sense of family—to sustain him. It's a loneliness he won't know he's feeling."

"In that case it won't bother him, will it?"

She refused Som's offer of his car and started walking. She

catalogued the packing she would have to do for Brij, who had not told her he was leaving. His motor car pictures, his chest expander, his collection of gadgets. And some of his clothes were at the *dhobi*. All the *Health and Strength* magazines and the muscle-men pasted on his cupboard would have to be packed too. There was no taxi in sight and she went on walking. "Even storming and screaming would have more meaning to a child than what you do." Raj made it sound like a deformity, shrivelling her guts and repelling others. But if a cripple was what she was, it was too late to change. Did no one in the world understand the quiet loving sanity that has no high or low? A taxi swung to the curb for her and she got in.

Brij was at the gate, on tenterhooks.

"Oh Mama, I forgot to tell you—"

"That you're leaving," she said and smiled.

"Yes," he looked relieved. "Papa just phoned to say I should come as soon as possible, right away if I can. The car is on its way."

"Come up and help me pack."

Brij lingered, tense and eager.

"The car'll be here any minute. Could you possibly send my stuff on afterwards?"

"Then send the car for it, will you?"

"I will." His face lit up. "There it is."

She saw him off and walked tiredly up the stairs to the refuge of her room. She opened the door. It gave her a shock to see Raj in her chair.

"Hello," he said.

"What are you doing here?"

"Waiting for you."

"I'd rather be alone."

"Then you've taken up with the wrong man."

224

She stood rigid and unyielding in his arms.

"The door is open," she objected.

"Let's leave it that way. Better still, let's go and make love under the open sky."

Simrit leaned against him. Slipping her arms round him under the rough tweed of his jacket she held him close, the tweed grazing her cheek, brushing her tears. She began to explain about Brij.

"I know," said Raj. "He was here telling me about it. He's happy and excited. Share it with him."

"I can't. It'll be wrong for him."

"It may be. But share it now. We'll face the other part later—together." He caressed the back of her neck. "How did it go about the Corpus?"

"Oh that," said Simrit, wiping her eyes on his handkerchief and sitting down. "We have to look after it so it doesn't get thin and weak. Feed it up. Give it a spit and a polish on Sundays—you know. *Safeguard* it was the word Som used."

"So we're just where we were."

"I'm afraid so," said Simrit.

Raj came back to the puzzle again.

"Whatever made Som stick a document like that on you? Revenge for what?"

Simrit frowned, "It wasn't revenge. It was just Som."

"'Just Som' is what I've been trying to get at," said Raj. "What was Som like?"

"Well he liked to have the last word. The terms were his parting shot, like his not sending the car for Merriwether."

"Not doing what?"

"After all, he had nothing against Merriwether. The amount of drinks we'd had off Merriwether, and I don't know how many times he'd been to our house and sent chocolates for the children. He was a perfectly likeable soul. He wasn't specially my cup of tea, but he and Som were getting on like a house on fire when Som decided out of the blue not to send the car for him. When Som behaved like that, unreasonably, or suddenly dropped someone we'd known quite well or even someone who'd been a blood brother to him, I'd feel uncomfortable about it but I wouldn't protest. I'd accept it. And then it happened to me."

"Think back, Simrit. There must have been some reason for this blow-up with Merriwether, whoever he was."

"Darling, what on earth does it matter now?"

"Pure interest," said Raj. "Of all the people I have never met, Som is quite the most fascinating."

"There was no reason at all. I think Som had to invent one so he could get on to the next proposition with a clear-ish conscience."

"He's magnificent," said Raj, "an uncommonly whole person, all of him there, or none of him. There's a kind of elemental grandeur about him. I've never come across anything quite like it. One meets much tamer types in everyday living."

"It's nice to see you lost in admiration over Som."

"He's superb—and real. Men like him bring progress and we haven't enough of them. If only they had feelings, too, progress wouldn't become a danger. About Merriwether, how did he react to the car not being sent?"

"Oh he told a mutual acquaintance at the Club after Som had left the Company that Som had the most atrocious manners."

"I suppose," said Raj, "that could be the answer to the puzzle. The Consent Terms are atrocious bad manners—no consideration for the other person."

"But that's not true," objected Simrit, thinking of her

life with Som, thinking of Merriwether, of Lalli, of Vetter. "He has such an enormous concern for the other person, so much of it, almost too much. Only 'the other person' changes."

"You're still in love with Som."

"Not after this Corpus he's hung on me."

"Even with that."

"Well we both are—a little."

If one was the kind of person who could not make savage breaks with the past, then one must carry it along, and how could one without loving it, or at least feeling friendly toward it?

22

Mr Shah's party at the Zodiac Room at the Intercontinental was as studded with the leading lights of government, officialdom and business—every man with his label and   every woman with her husband's—as his party weeks earlier   had been, but with a difference.   Simrit stood confidently near Raj.   No cut-outs in her with an icy wind blowing through. Oddly, Raj who had b̧een as elated as a schoolboy at   last month's party was watchful and serious.   He was, she knew, making plans.   He was probably in next week already, a man with a mission.

When Sumer Singh, the guest of honour came in, there

was a noticeable movement through the room, as if a draught had blown onto a toy stage, scattered the cardboard actors and set them down in different places. There was no mistaking Sumer Singh's importance now. In Delhi the throng gravitated instinctively toward the seat of power, as if it could smell it. Power, that way, rather resembled roasting meat, thought Simrit, enticing the appetite for miles around. Shah's own sober recognition of it was this party for the man with whose Ministry he had done business and who had become the Foreign Minister in last week's reshuffle. For the first time an active interest in the people around her stirred Simirt.

"How are you feeling?" Raj asked in a low voice.

"Wonderful."

"How's the disinfectant smell. Powerful as ever I hope?"

"Yes; absolutely."

He reached down for her hand and pressed it hard against him.

"I'm glad to hear it because you're going to need your certainty and your wits about you. We all are."

"This evening?" she bantered.

"Every day from now on."

Simrit made a moue of distaste. "That sounds sombre."

"It is."

She did not have to ask him why. He had talked of little else in the past few days. There would have to be a planned campaign among those who cared, through the press, through contacts at every level, if they were going to keep the freedoms they had so long and lazily taken for granted. When the Eastern alliance became official policy no one could be sure what basic changes would come, how everyday life would be affected. An avalanche in dribbles, in fancy dress, Raj had called it. Personally she couldn't quite believe it. It was too far-fetched. Of course life would remain the same as ever—more or less. This was India. And what did it matter if some changes came as long as she and Raj were together? Anyway, where were the ominous signs? The signs seen and unseen, enveloped Raj.

"Revolutions don't begin with an announcement."

"That much I had gathered," said Simrit.

"When you begin to see the signs it's already half complete."

And then one day there's a strike in some corner, in a place no one ever heard of before, that becomes more than a strike or a take-over of a plant or a vital installation, or perhaps, he mused, mutiny in a port three-quarters of the way down the east coastline.

"What made you say that?" she interrupted.

"I don't know, I'm guessing. But that's how these things happen. And the invisible events have paved the way, the small clamps and threats becoming imperceptibly bigger—on criticism, on expression. A general feeling of uneasiness nagging one. You're a writer. You ought to understand atmosphere. And before you know it you're a helpless spectator."

"I don't know where you keep your ear, but it isn't to the ground. Raj, this is India—"

"You keep saying that."

"—and no one wants violent revolution here. We've already had our own kind in our fight for freedom."

"It wasn't enough, Simrit. It didn't involve enough people deeply enough or long enough. For that apparently we have to pay a price. And the price may be terror and a rigid system."

"No," she insisted, "positively no."

Raj's smile was strained.

"Tell that to the jobless and the hungry."

"The way you talk sometimes, I think you justify the terror you say is coming. What do you believe in?"

"In justice," he said grimly, "and it is terrible to believe in gentleness as well—in circumstances that no longer seem able to combine the two."

Through those arguments she had an inkling of what her relationship with him would be. It would never be a private, exclusive haven. Tomorrow Raj might be off to his constituency or on tour. And his work would always come first, getting the utter concentration men kept for the causes they served. But she would be part of the process. He was introducing her to people he wanted her to meet, turning to her every little while to make sure she was there. She would not be allowed to sit on the sidelines in this partnership.

After an hour of this Simrit urged, "Let's leave. And let's drop in at Ram Krishan's before we go home."

Raj consulted his watch and looked briefly round him, checking if there was anything more he could accomplish here.

"All right," he agreed doubtfully.

Simrit took his arm. "You've spoken to every single person you know and some besides. You can't do any more here."

Ram Krishan came to the door himself, shuffling in warm red slippers.

"Come in, you two."

The fire in the grate was dying. He had been reading in his favourite lumpy chair near it. He put another log on. Raj reached for Simrit's hand and held it securely in his.

"We are going to get married," he announced.

Simrit's questioning glance leapt to his. They had not even discussed it. What in the world was he talking about? Marriage—that was still a barrelful of problems away. She had expected they would come to it later, after taxes and children and a hundred and one other hurdles had been crossed. Besides, all these earth-shaking decisions were supposed to be hers to make, of her own free will, in her own good time. Raj was the one who had insisted on that. And she wanted time, in any case, to understand what had happened to her.

"As soon as possible," Raj added emphatically.

Ram Krishan glanced from one to the other and shuffled into the next room for whisky and glasses. The mild food of friendship was all very well, but tonight there was a live current connecting them, bright lights dancing. The beginning he had watched had come to fruition. And holy matrimony was the true and ancient answer to the holiest of God's gifts. Raj's eyes on his woman were those of a man in charge. Funny boy, Raj. When he finally got landed it had to be with a woman who had hordes of children and a tax problem the size of a python embracing her. That was the trouble with being brought up on challenges. No simple straightforward domesticity for him. And for her obviously, poverty, or at least austerity, had a powerful mental attraction. Well the two of them would find out soon enough, but after all the finding out might not damage them in the richer experience of a struggle shared. As he got more ice cubes out of the try Ram Krishan thought: Courage is the most moving thing in the world and these two have plenty of the foolhardy brand.

Simrit jumped into accusation the minute Ram Krishan left. "You said I didn't need a man for identity—or status."

"Ah but you do for other grosser—and finer—reasons," Raj pointed out. "Anyway you need me. And I had to announce it before a witness to make sure there's no backsliding. A Hindu needs to be pinned down."

Raj lit a cigarette, threw the match in the fire and said, "There's another reason that may not appeal to your academic mind."

"What?"

"A husband and wife lie down together at the end of each day."

There was enduring comradeship in the sentence and the way he said it.

Ram Krishan came back and poured their drinks.

"What about the Corpus?" he asked.

"To hell with the Corpus," said Raj amiably.

'I'm not sending the Corpus to any hell," retorted Ram Krishan. "It's what brought Simrit to this house. Here's to it."

He raised his glass in solemn toast. Then, all at once he made an admiring little speech about Raj. Afterwards, putting his glass down he took Simrit's face in his hands and touched his lips to her forehead. The three of them stood awkwardly, eyes moist, faces flushed, not trusting themselves to speak. The emotional moment passed.

"Well," Ram Krishan wiped his glasses on his handkerchief, "what is happening in the wide world?"

"We've just been to a party to celebrate Sumer Singh becoming Foreign Minister."

"So," said Ram Krishan and sat down.

The silence with only an occasional spark and crackle from the grate was full of the men's tacit understanding and agreement.

Simrit burst out, "It's too ridiculous. Nothing's going to happen. Everything will go on as usual."

Neither of the men said a word.

"Retribution catches up," said Ram Krishan at last, "with people who do not face a problem. Religions are supposed to help one face up. Religions are like public schools. Each produces a type, a uniform personality. The type ours produces doesn't face up—it puts problems into cold storage. Oh yes, it keeps things in an excellent state of preservation, perfect museum pieces." He looked at Raj with a light in his eyes, "But I've found a way out of that."

"Have you?"

Ram Krishan nodded.

"The way out is a matter of perspective and proportion. Philosophy, have you noticed, is a little like architecture. Proportion makes the difference between a stunted distorted structure and a good, beautiful, useful one."

"No, we hadn't noticed," said Raj.

He drew Simrit down on the sofa beside him and put an arm around her.

"To fight wrong," Ram Krishan went on, "a man has to believe it is terribly important to fight it. However unimportant it might be in eternity or a hundred years hence, it has to matter *today*. That is the point to dig out of the Hindu approach, move it out of the universal into the present. The ingredients of the approach are already there, rather buried down under at the moment, like the best of diamonds. We have to dig them up, highlight them, make it known that this too is Hinduism. It's this that will provide the stamina, the sticking point, the boiling point we need to resist what we don't believe in, and give us the will to act. We had it under Gandhi. He took *ahimsa*—non-violence—Hinduism's oldest idea and sent a whole nation into battle with nothing but that. Who would have thought it possible? You in your generation may have to find a different springboard, but there's no scarcity of ideas among us. Find the one that will bring the best in men to the surface and you'll have an unbeatable combine."

Raj said dryly, "Well, professor, that's the problem, isn't t? Which is the famous, workable idea that will lead us out of our tribulations? Not country. Marx abolished frontiers when he united the working classes. No one will buy it any more, beyond a point, certainly not the young. Not nonviolence either. That would take another Gandhi to promote. So where is it, the touchstone that will work today?"

"There has never been any touchstone except character and example," said Ram Krishan. "Any ism under the sun needs that to enthuse and inspire. It takes a Christ, a Lenin, a Mao. Unfortunately—or fortunately—humanity needs inspiration to move it even half a step out of the rut. Inspiration draws it out, but what sustains the momentum is an idea that people believe in and are willing to work for."

"And I'm asking you what that is—for us—today."

"Can I tell you that?" said Ram Krishan "Get this or any nation thinking and it will think its way into an answer."

"Philosophers have such a lot of time," sighed Raj. "For the rest of us it may already be too late."

"To think?" said Ram Krishan amused.

He was so amused he burst into a long low chuckle, thoroughly enjoying the sound of his own mirth.

"Raj, you look positively offended," he ended cheerfully.

"It's Hinduism in a nutshell," lamented Raj. "Here we are faced with a crisis of enormous proportion. My woman here says it isn't happening at all, and you, my mentor, tell me to sit back and think about it."

"The crisis is there in the first place because we haven't thought," retorted Ram Krishan, "and even in crisis, especially in crisis, we must think. It was never much use acting first and using one's brain afterward. And," he continued softly, precisely, tapping the arm of his chair, "to get back to my earlier point, to build Jerusalem you have to come back to character. Not iron on the outside goading men to their tasks, but iron in the soul that produces real men in the first place. Are we really so bankrupt that we haven't such men, one single such man?"

Raj rubbed his face with his hands.

"Well," he said wearily, "whatever happens, I suppose we'll carry on living. As to the rest—"

He left the sentence in the air. A sudden slackening of his shoulders, a droop of his head, gave him a listless defeated look so uncharacteristic that Simrit protested anxiously.

"I can't bear it when you're not on top of the world, battling Nemesis."

Raj went on, "It isn't even as though we were young and had all our lives ahead of us to put wrongs right."

Simrit looked past the man slumped in his chair to the born fighter she knew he was. Life was never long enough to overthrow all the tyrants. Whose life was long enough to put everything right? What was more, the biggest crisis sometimes found one old, or at least no longer young. It gave more power to living, to loving. She thought of herself led to Raj in full-blown maturity. She would not have had the discovery of Raj happen sooner for anything. From this high spot an immense valley of choices spread out before her gaze and she felt free at last to choose what her life would be. She was filled with the sheer rightness of being alive and healthy at this particular time. Part of it was physical wellbeing, as if there was no effort she could not ask of her body. The rest was balanced in a deeper, calmer rejoicing.

As for Raj—Raj was going to leave his mark and nothing could stop it. His tradition was public service. He didn't know any other. Men like him were born to lead and educate, sometimes to triumph just when it seemed fortunes could go no lower. Raj would be all right.

Printed in the United States
125180LV00001B/19/A

9 780393 332223